POST-HUMAN

DAVID SIMPSON

POST-HUMAN

Copyright © 2009 David Simpson

All rights reserved.

Cover illustration by Jennifer Simpson
Interior design and layout by Jennifer Simpson

ISBN: **1481808834**
ISBN-13: **978-1481808835**

www.post-humannovel.com
Give feedback on the book at:
posthumanmedia@gmail.com

ACKNOWLEDGMENTS

Thank you to my editor, Autumn J. Conley, for being so thorough, creative, and awesome.

Thank you to everyone who has read this book and the series and told someone else about it. Thank you to those who reviewed it positively on Amazon. The series is the huge hit that it is today because of you. You made a guy's dreams come true.

Thank you to my wife Jennifer for putting as much work into this book as I have. From the cover, to the formatting, to the promotion, to the endless technical headaches that arise on an almost daily basis, you are the magic that lets this be. You're the greatest wife in the universe and all other universes as well.

PART 1

Any sufficiently advanced technology is indistinguishable from magic. **—Arthur C. Clarke**

1

WAKING UP was not something one had to work very hard to accomplish these days; like most things, it was done for you. The nanobots, also known as *nans*, were set to awaken their host at whatever time he or she desired. They would always, however, awaken their host just before the end of the most recent REM sleep so that the host would arise alert and feeling well rested. It was usually easy to remember one's dreams, too, and recounting dreams to friends, loved ones, and co-workers had become a universal pre-noon activity; after noon was a different story, as by that point, it was considered a *faux pas* to continue discussing a dream—best just to let it go and focus on the real world. Sleep was hardly "death's counterfeit" any longer, as Shakespeare had suggested, but rather, an important source of entertainment. Early-morning remembrances of fantastic dreams, in addition to one's high level of alertness, made it difficult to wake up feeling anything other than optimistic—difficult, but not impossible.

James Keats opened his eyes and sat up in bed. He turned to his right, looked out his window, and saw that the sun had risen, yet the summer sky was blotted out by low-hanging gray clouds hovering like a dull blanket just above the skyline of the city. He turned to his left and saw his wife Katherine, still fast asleep. She wouldn't awaken for another hour, just after he would've already left for work. She could've set herself to wake up with him. This was her plan—deafening silence. He wondered when his punishment would end, but part of him knew it never would. Their love was over.

James turned from her and sighed as he lifted the heated blanket from his legs and stepped out onto the heated carpet of his bedroom. Just a few short steps away were his bathroom and the promise of his morning shower. He opened his *mind's eye* and selected a soft spray at a comfortable forty-five degrees Celsius. When he stepped into the shower, the spray hit him from four directions, and he relaxed against the kneading fingers of the water.

People in the industrialized world had been enjoying their morning showers for two centuries now, though there were more efficient ways of cleaning oneself; on Mars, James had used a microwave shower that detected foreign substances in a matter of a few seconds and removed them from the body. The process of removing dirt and oil was over just as quickly as it began, but James hated it. The technology had been available for years, but it had never caught on with the general population. A traditional shower was a luxury too valuable to give up. Even if it took a few extra minutes in the morning, the hot water and massaging jets were like an old friend to humanity.

People were funny that way—the way they would resist the future and cling to the past. It was like how the concept of a god had never left the species. Very few people alive believed in a god—there was no longer a need to—yet the phrases, "oh my God" or "dear God," were still commonly used. It was as if people needed those phrases, those concepts from the past, to help them understand the future.

As James shampooed his hair, he reactivated his mind's eye and checked his phone messages; there were none. He quickly checked his e-mail, but there was nothing interesting. His older brother had sent him some pornographic holoprograms to keep him company, but he didn't open them—maybe later. At the moment, he wasn't in the mood. He set the shower to end in five seconds and selected a towel-off of forty degrees Celsius, to begin the moment the shower stopped.

As warm air replaced the water, blowing through the vents and quickly drying him, his thoughts drifted back to Katherine. Why wouldn't she listen? He'd done nothing wrong—at least, nothing physically wrong.

It's what you wanted to do that hurts me, James, she said.

But I can't control what I want to do—I can only control what I actually do, he told her.

And we both know why you didn't 'actually' do anything, don't we? Don't we?

She had a point.

After he finished in the shower, James dressed quickly in his standard-issue black uniform. He pulled on the t-shirt and flight pants, then slipped into his flight jacket with the NASA emblem emblazoned on the right shoulder. He walked out of the bedroom, casting one last look at the back of his wife's head, her blonde hair the only evidence of an actual person in the room with him.

He floated down to the first floor gently and hovered into the kitchen, making a soft landing on the linoleum floor. He opened his mind's eye once again and activated his food replicator. From the breakfast menu, he selected a poached egg on a bagel, served hot, and a large orange juice, served cold. The food was ready in an instant, and he gulped down his orange juice, deciding to eat the bagel on the way.

He slipped on his flight boots and selected the *door open* icon in his mind's eye. Then he stepped on his front lawn and gazed across the water at the downtown core of Vancouver. It was rush hour, and thousands of bodies buzzed above the city. On a good day, he would look at that sight and think of honeybees working on the comb. Today, however, the sight reminded him of flies buzzing around a pile of excrement or a rotting corpse. The sky was brown above the massive skyscrapers and all across the horizon, as though a painter had soiled his thumb and rubbed it across the expanse of what could have been a masterpiece.

James took two quick bites of his bagel and placed the rest in the pocket of his jacket. He pulled on his helmet and looked skyward as he lifted off from his lawn and slowly approached the low-hanging clouds. He liked to take a moment or two before activating his magnetic field. He enjoyed the way the wind felt as he picked up speed on his ascent. As he entered the clouds and began to feel the temperature dropping, he activated the protective field; it produced a greenish light that encapsulated his body. Once the magnetic field was in place, he was free to bolt upward, unhindered by friction, air pressure, temperature, or anything else. In seconds, he was above the stratosphere, using his mind's eye to plot an automatic course for Venus.

The trip there usually took just under an hour—still one of the longest daily commutes of anyone in the solar system. People regularly commuted between hemispheres on Earth, and some even commuted between the Earth and the moon, but very few commuted interplanetarily. After plotting his course, he bolted forward once again, this time at an even faster rate than before.

As he passed by the moon and breathed the compressed air released by his flight suit, he surfed the Net, as was his customary commuting routine. First, he would check sports. The Vancouver Canucks had lost to an expansion team on Mars; the players blamed the difference in gravity and promised a better performance back on Earth. "Damn. Lost that bet," James cursed to himself.

Next, he checked the mainstream news. NBC was interviewing James's boss, Inua Colbe, executive assistant to the president of A.I. governance. The interviewer was sitting across from Colbe, dangling her pointed dress shoe from her foot and smiling as she asked him questions in front of a welcoming fireplace.

"There have been a lot of questions about the delay between upgrades, Dr. Colbe. Can you tell us why it has taken over five years for this latest upgrade to be approved?"

Colbe smiled as he answered. The camera closed in on his smiling face; his pearly white teeth could distract anyone from what was being said, putting them at ease. "The simple fact is that this upgrade is far better than any that have been uploaded in the past. It offers more disease resistance, an increase in muscle tone, and improvements to the cardiovascular system that should increase energy. Then, of course, there is the benefit everyone is talking about."

"The IQ increase," the interviewer stated, finishing Inua's thought.

"That's right. An increase in neuron growth, specifically targeting spindle cells, which we are forecasting will lead to an eight-point jump in IQ for the average citizen—the biggest jump in history."

IQ measurements were based on the numbers from before the nans had first started slowly improving the population's intelligence. An IQ of 100 was no longer the average IQ of a population, since almost everyone alive was now at the same level. There were only a few people who were naturally above the standard level—James was one of them.

"I think people are very much looking forward to the IQ portion of the download. I know that I certainly am."

"Aren't we all?" Colbe interjected.

"But why not increase the IQ slowly? We've been used to annual improvements of a point or two. Why was there a five-year gap followed suddenly by this huge leap forward?"

Colbe smiled again, this time nodding to show that he understood the concerns of the general public.

He's a great PR man, thought James, *because he's a phony bastard.*

"Well, Keiko, what people have to understand is that as the IQ of the general public increases, it becomes more and more difficult to provide upgrades—not impossible, mind you, but more difficult. In the early days, it was very easy to find countless bright subjects to study so that we could learn a great deal about what structures in their brains facilitated their intelligence. However, once we started getting into the numbers we are entering now, where the IQ of the general public is 149 and about to reach 157, the number of subjects who are *naturally* this intelligent—those on whom we can model the upgrades—diminishes significantly. Unlike previous upgrades, this particular one isn't based on a large number of people. Rather, it is actually based on one person, a man named James Keats who is the commander of the terraforming project on Venus, and who happens to have an IQ above 200."

James opened his mouth in shock. "He screwed me. He...screwed me."

"My goodness! An IQ above 200 naturally! That's astounding!"

"He's an astounding individual, Keiko. He's only thirty-six years old and is commanding a team of scientists, some of whom are three times his age, on one of the most important projects of our time. He played an integral part in the terraforming of Mars, and he was the only real candidate for the job on Venus. In addition, he was generous enough to offer scans of his brain to the A.I. so this latest upgrade could be modeled on him. He's a great citizen."

James blinked, still shocked to be listening to Colbe talk about him during a live broadcast. "That asshole," he said out loud before using his mind's eye to dial Colbe's phone. Obviously Colbe wouldn't answer as he was busy being Judas, so James waited for Colbe's answering message to appear. An old message popped up; it was probably recorded several years ago, judging by the passé clothes Colbe was wearing. He looked the same, as the nans had kept him young; if anything, he looked a little better now.

When the image on Inua's machine stopped speaking and the *beep* indicated that James was free to leave his message, he spoke in as cordial a tone as he could muster, but he was pissed. "Inua, I am watching you tell the populated solar system that their new brains are going to be modeled after mine. I thought we had a deal, Inua. I thought you said I would be anonymous. I don't want reporters asking me questions. I don't want everyone in the solar system looking at me like I'm related to them. Was I not clear about this?"

With that, he terminated the message and stopped the broadcast. He thought of surfing the Net some more to take his mind off of his irritation, but he decided not to. Instead, he would work. He opened the file containing the computer model of that day's experiment. He ran it through from beginning to end, but couldn't pay attention to it; he was too preoccupied with trying to convince himself not to be angry. *There's no reason to be this upset*, he told himself, but yet there it was. Why was he so angry? Why didn't he want people to know about him? What was it about the upgrade that was upsetting him so much? Why was he afraid of connection?

2

With a 600-degree Celsius surface, Venus might have been hell, but James wouldn't have had it any other way. His favorite part of the day was his approach to the planet and subsequent descent into the atmosphere.

It was roughly the same size as Earth, with only a few hundred kilometers separating them in diameter, but that was one of the few similarities it shared with its sister planet. Its atmosphere consisted almost entirely of carbon dioxide, and the resulting greenhouse effect made it the hottest planet in the solar system. The deadly heat made the existence of water on the planet impossible, but there was rain—a deadly sulfuric acid that combined with the heat to make Venus as inhospitable a place as any in the solar system—just the sort of challenge on which James thrived.

Once he reached the Venusian stratosphere, James set a course for the research lab on the surface. He smiled as he entered the thick, dark clouds and blasted through the acid and heat.

On the surface, in the research lab that was not so affectionately referred to as "The Oven" by the workers who inhabited it, Thel Cleland looked up from her work on the magnetic propeller and watched a tiny blue dot in her mind's eye—the dot that signified the approach of Commander Keats. She had taken it upon herself to be there to personally greet him when he arrived that morning, so she'd been watching for him for the last ten minutes. "Look sharp, everybody. The boss is coming!" she announced to her two fellow workers as they prepared for the morning's experiment.

"The boss?" replied Djanet Dove, smiling to herself.

Rich Borges smiled too.

It was difficult to think of Commander Keats as a "boss." He was young, friendly, caring, and a pleasure to work with.

Thel stood and floated gently up toward the airlock. She was a tall, slender, dark-haired woman with a strong, athletic build. There was a certain unmistakable self-confidence in her every move, every gesture, every stance. At fifty, she felt she finally knew how to live; she'd earned her self-assurance. Of course, as with everyone else, the nans had kept her young—biologically, she was twenty-nine, and men of all ages pursued her relentlessly. She knew what she was looking for, though. She knew *exactly* what she was looking for.

The greenish glow of James's magnetic field was visible for an instant before he emerged from the cloud cover. Weather moved slowly on Venus—there was rarely anything to obscure one's view on the surface, and Thel was able to watch Commander Keats—James—completely unobscured as he approached the outer magnetic doors. Once inside, he disengaged his magnetic field and opened the airlock door.

Thel floated before him, smiling as he removed his helmet. She laughed and covered her mouth.

"What?" James asked, surprised.

Thel reached out and wiped the corner of his lip with the tip of her finger. "You've got egg on your face this morning, Commander."

"Oh...thanks," he said, his face coloring.

"No problem, Commander."

James struggled to look into her eyes; it was difficult to look at her—she seemed able to look right through him, right into his soul. Did she know what he was thinking?

But I can't control what I want to do—I can only control what I actually do.

He turned away for a moment and noticed Rich and Djanet watching—not working—watching. "Uh...preparations are going okay, I hope?"

Thel noticed the changed look on James's face and turned to see her coworkers as they sneaked quick glances upward, trying to look as though they weren't looking. Her smile broadened. "Just fine, Commander. We'll be ready."

"Good, good. I...uh...I better go get ready." James began to float across the lab toward the second-story doorway to his office but stopped when he noticed another greenish light emerging from the clouds. "Hey...it's Old-timer!"

Old-timer, formerly known as Craig Emilson, arrived on the exact same trajectory as James had a minute earlier. He was dressed in an identical flight suit, as all the researchers were, and only his extra ten centimeters in height prevented dizzying déjà vu. After Old-timer entered the airlock and slipped off his helmet, he smiled at Thel, kissed her on the cheek, and vigorously shook hands with James. "Hey, good buddy!" Old-timer said, offering his usual, very familiar greeting.

"Good morning, pal!" replied James.

Old-timer had the polar opposite effect on James that Thel did; somehow, *he* put the younger man at ease. He was self-assured, just as Thel was, but there was something different.

"Too bad about those Canucks of yours, eh, Jimmy?"

"I'm impressed, Old-timer. It took you all of four seconds to bring that up."

"Well, I'm not one for beating around the bush, especially when it comes to collecting on a wager. You owe me."

"I know, I know. I didn't forget."

"What did you bet?" Thel inquired.

Old-timer and James exchanged glances.

"Would you like to tell her, or shall I?" asked Old-timer.

"I wouldn't dare deprive you of your chance to gloat. The honor is yours."

"Thank you, sir," Old-timer responded, performing an exaggerated bow. "Commander Keats has agreed to join me this evening for...are you ready, Thel?"

"What is it?"

"For a beer!"

Thel gasped in mock astonishment. "I can't believe it! You got *him* to agree to have a drink! I've been trying to get him to have a drink with me for three years!"

"Well, we can thank a certain Martian expansion hockey team for this miracle!"

"I still can't believe they lost," James said, almost pouting.

"Oh, c'mon! Don't look so down, champ! You'll enjoy it! The nans will fix up those brain cells overnight! I promise, you won't do a speck of damage to that noggin of yours."

"Is that why you don't drink, Commander? Afraid you might lose an IQ point?" Thel asked in jest.

"I just don't see the appeal. I like thinking. I enjoy it. Why would anyone purposefully impair their ability to do it?"

Old-timer and Thel looked at each other for a moment before they burst out laughing. "Hopefully you'll find out at the pub with me tonight," Old-timer replied before adding, "You ready to fire up the *Zeus* this morning?"

"Can't wait."

Old-timer, like everyone else, was twenty-nine biologically, but he was chronologically 110—the only centenarian on the team. He moved like a young man and had the libido of a young man, but one could tell after only a few moments in his presence that he was a senior. Something seemed to happen to people once they reached a certain age: They seemed to recapture their joy of life, and they often got along best with the younger generations.

"Are you ready, Old-timer?" Thel asked.

"You know I am always ready for an-y-thing," he replied, leaning in toward the younger woman, putting his arm around her and raising his eyebrow saucily. Only Old-timer could take such liberties with her.

"Well, I'll leave you two alone," James said, smiling. "I'll be in my office for a few minutes. We'll commence at 9:30 a.m. Pacific. Let everyone know." James met Thel's eyes one last time; she could still see through him.

Inside his office, James removed his flight jacket and set his helmet down next to his desk. The office was sparsely decorated, with just a desk in the middle of the room and a couple of chairs. He meant to replicate a plant, but kept forgetting. He hoped Thel would pick one out for him, since she likely had better taste than he did.

A sudden flash appeared in the corner of his vision, activating his mind's eye. It was Inua Colbe, returning his call. James sighed when he saw the other man and took a moment to collect himself before responding flatly, "Keats here."

"James? James, I just watched a rather unpleasant message on my phone. What's the matter with you?"

"I could ask you the same thing. You used my name on a broadcast."

"And?"

"I know how they think, Inua. I know how the mind works. I know how it works better than anyone. They'll feel a connection to me, and I don't want that."

"Calm down, James. Calm."

James folded his arms.

Inua reassessed. "How long has it been since we've been golfing together?"

"Two years," James replied, sitting down behind his desk.

"Two years? Two years? Holy...that time with our wives in Arizona? That was—"

"Yes, two years."

"My, how time flies. Listen, we should go again."

"Golf? Please tell me you have something better to offer than that."

"I'm not offering anything," Inua said, suddenly indignant. "Remember, James, I'm the guy that got you Venus."

"What's that supposed to mean?"

"You know, there are still a lot of prominent people down here who want you removed. A faction in the Governing Council thinks the Hektor plan is more practical than yours."

James smiled. "I agree. Without question, the Hektor plan is a much more practical way of blowing up Venus. On the other hand, if you want to terraform her—"

"You're being belligerent."

"Then fire me, Inua."

"Look, all I am saying is there are a lot of people down here with multiple PhDs who disagree with you."

"But *you* agree with me. The Hektor plan is lunacy, and you know it. Smashing an asteroid into Venus to get rid of the atmosphere isn't going to accomplish anything other than destroying the planet. You have to have a little more finesse than that, Inua. Jesus Christ! You know this."

"I did you a favor. Don't bust my balls just because I needed you to do me a favor in return."

"I've done enough favors. All I asked was that I remain anonymous. Was that too much to ask?"

A new strategy flashed into Inua's eyes. "What are you afraid of, James? You're afraid you'll be famous for a little while?"

"Exactly."

"Let me let you in on a little secret. Fame is a sham—a total sham. It's spectacle. No one who's famous deserves it. They're only famous because the public needs to believe that there are people worth idolizing—it's the malady of the herd."

"I know this, Inua."

"Do you? That's interesting. And do you also know we're forecasting a 210 IQ for the general public within a decade?"

James did not respond.

"That's right. 210. The people will have reached *your* level."

"Based on my model?"

"Based on your model. You. The man who knows fame is a sham. Do you think the general public will care about you then, once you're just like them?"

For the first time in his life, James felt the need to throw up.

"You're going to live forever, James. Up against forever, ten years of fame won't seem like much."

"No. No it won't."

"There. You see?" Inua was smiling now. "Even with that big soppy brain of yours, old Inua can still teach you a thing or two. Now try to relax, my friend, and try enjoy the notoriety, okay? And let's make sure we get together for some golf soon—maybe next week, once people are used to the new upgrade and the PR tour is over. What do you say?"

"I-I hate golf. I'll take you to a hockey game."

Inua laughed—it was hollow—a salesman's laugh. "Okay, old friend. Okay. Goodbye."

The connection was severed. James swiveled his chair around and faced the glass wall behind his desk. Outside was dark, hot hell.

James glided out of his office and toward the central dome of the lab. There, the other four members of the research team were sitting together near the base of the MP—the four-story tall magnetic propeller that stood in the middle of the lab. It was about twice as thick as the coast redwood trees near his house in Vancouver and built primarily of titanium. Old-timer had taken to calling it *Zeus* and the name was appropriate; it was worthy of the gods. James activated his mind's eye and quickly saw that the rest of the team was already signed in and were ready to begin monitoring the test run.

"Feeling lucky, Commander?" Rich called up from his seat next to the other researchers.

"Who needs luck when you have math?" James replied, jokingly.

"Who needs luck when we have *you*?" said Thel.

James smiled.

So many things seemed to be wrong in his life. He wasn't sure exactly what they were—there was just a feeling—like something was slipping away. It wore on him.

Zeus sustained him. These moments made him happy. To accomplish something—something amazing—that sustained him.

His life had not been like other people's. In a time when infants were born into the world with every genetic advantage known to science, James was exceptional. No one had isolated the genes that could create someone like him—at least not yet.

At the age of six, he designed his first robot. At the age of seven, he designed one that could translate French into English. By the time he was ten, he had programmed it to learn other languages and it became the first speaking universal translator on Earth. The robot was confiscated by the A.I. Governing Council later that year—only one A.I. was allowed to function on Earth—but the Council took note of its young designer, and were quick to put him to work.

James was offered a position in any government field he desired, and he chose terraforming. At that time, the terraforming of the moon was well underway, but a Martian project seemed decades, if not centuries, down the road. James changed all that when he invented the SRS—the Self-Replicating System. He designed dense programs for robots that would blast off to another planet and reproduce. *"Adam"* was sent to Mars when James was only fourteen. By the time James was sixteen, Adam had used the available resources on the planet to reproduce 100 times. The resulting work force built a research lab that was ready for human inhabitants the following year. James began commuting to Mars soon thereafter and, only five years later, Mars had been terraformed. Now, fifteen years after the terraforming was complete, Mars had its own city—its own hockey team—and the bastards had beaten the Canucks.

Venus was a whole other matter—a planet that could be the jewel of the solar system if only its harsh atmosphere could be removed. The scientists on the Governing Council had their hopes set on a plan that had been designed almost half a century earlier. They wanted to use nuclear detonations to knock the Hektor asteroid into Venus, the theory being that the resulting explosion would destroy the carbon dioxide atmosphere. Then the crackpots wanted to attach a gigantic rocket onto Jupiter's moon, IO, and send it on a quarter-century long trip to Venus, where it would act as a sunshield and allow for the cooling of the planet. The whole process would take a century.

James's success on Mars killed their plan, making it look needlessly elaborate in comparison. Now the pressure was on him to prove that his Venus idea could succeed as well, delivering results that were faster and better than those proposed by the Governing Council's top minds. The first step was to send an SRS to the planet—it built the lab and the Zeus. The Zeus functioned on the same principles as the magnetic implants in everyone's spinal cords; these implants created a magnetic propulsion and generated the protective fields that allowed people to fly—even through space. The Zeus would generate this same magnetic energy but would spin it like a propeller, creating a massive fan, thus forcing the atmosphere of Venus into space. The Zeus James would activate that day was just a prototype—a baby. If it functioned properly, James would signal the go-ahead to the SRS robots still on the surface to build another Zeus—one two kilometers high and the width of a football field, with the capability of removing the Venusian atmosphere in a matter of months.

It just needed to work today.

"Whenever you're ready, James," Old-timer said, smiling up at his young friend.

James was still floating about a dozen feet above the floor of the lab. "Okay. This is it. Keep your eyes on those meters. The numbers have to line up exactly as they do in the simulation. If you see anything amiss, you have permission to engage shut down. Everybody copy?"

"Aye, Aye, Cap'n," replied Rich. The others likewise assented, albeit without Rich's unnecessary seafaring pirate accent.

"Okay then. Let's do it."

The Zeus began to spin. It moved without noise, floating on magnetic energy. It quickly began to pick up steam. Before long, the movement caused the air in the lab to circulate into a breeze.

"Mmm...feels kind of nice," Rich commented.

"Concentrate, guys," James said, still looking straight up through the tinted roof of the dome.

The clouds were clearly starting to swirl. It was a magnificent sight. The clouds moved so slowly on Venus—to see them swirl as though a prairie summer storm were about to break sent chills down James's spine.

"The momentum is right on track, boss," Old-timer reported. "It's exactly to the computer model—to the decimal point."

"It has to be. I don't want to take any—"

Suddenly, there was a flash of light—a crack of energy that went through James's body before he lost consciousness. In the last second before he blacked out, he knew he was falling.

4

WAKING UP was suddenly a very difficult thing to do. Never in James's life had he felt groggy before—his head ached—it was a frightening feeling. He knew pain—everyone felt pain from time to time. People couldn't avoid the occasional spill every now and then, but the nans would release endorphins to minimize the pain and, whatever minor damage might be caused, be it a scraped knee or a bloody nose, was quickly repaired. This was different—this was a whole new experience.

James felt pain throughout most of his body; in his neck, in his back, and it shot down his legs—even his eyes hurt. He was looking straight up, through the dome. The clouds were still moving, but they had slowed considerably. He turned his head a little to the right to see that the Zeus had stopped spinning. "Thel? Old-timer?"

There was no response from the team.

Like a turtle on its back, he rocked his body from side to side to facilitate a turn onto his right side. He quickly regained his bearings; he had landed on a table, denting it with the impact of his body. He struggled to his feet and opened his mind's eye, but nothing happened. "My God. I'm offline."

He limped across the lab, past the now lifeless Zeus, and to his four friends. Each was unconscious, either slumped over in their chairs or sprawled on the floor. The first one he went to was Thel. "Thel? Thel!"

She began to stir.

"Can you hear me?"

She opened her eyes, but James could see the pain with which she did so. She groaned. "Wh-what happened?"

"Just relax for a second. Everything is okay, Thel. Just relax."

Djanet began to move, quickly followed by Old-timer. James called over to both of them as he lightly stroked Thel's face. "Are you guys okay?"

"What the hell—" Djanet began.

"I know this feeling," said Old-timer. "This is exactly what a hangover used to feel like, way back when."

"Oh my God!" Djanet suddenly exclaimed. "I'm offline!"

"We all are," James replied. He left Thel and attended to Rich, who was just beginning to regain consciousness.

"What happened?" Thel asked.

"I remember a flash," Old-timer said, struggling to develop a hypothesis. "I think our synapses might have been overloaded."

"Electrical charge?"

"But where did it come from?" asked Djanet.

"I don't know," James answered.

"The numbers were normal," Old-timer reported as he rubbed a bruise on his elbow.

"Anyone notice how hot it's getting in here?" Rich said, still groggy.

"Oh no—the whole lab is offline!" Djanet realized.

"Don't panic," Old-timer said, suddenly showing his hard-won wisdom and maturity.

"Our nans must have been overloaded by the blast. The connection is severed—everything in the lab has shut down," Thel concluded.

"The airlocks aren't run by computer, and neither is the air circulation system. We're okay, but it's going to get hot in here, real fast," Old-timer answered.

James walked away from Rich and lifted off into the air. He stopped, hovering about five feet above the others. "Looks like we're going to be fine. The flight systems are still operational."

"Oh thank God," Rich began. "I thought I was going to have to get used to a new life as a roasted entrée!"

"How can the flight systems still be operational if everything was overloaded?" Djanet asked.

"They're larger systems. Each individual nan is its own microscopic computer. A surge of electricity that's powerful enough to knock a human unconscious is powerful enough to severely damage a nan. The flight systems, luckily, were able to absorb the surge, and since they are intranet systems rather than Internet systems, we can still access them," James answered.

"I thought we didn't need luck!" Rich retorted.

"We did today," Old-timer replied. "Math just didn't cut it."

"How did this happen, Commander?" Djanet asked.

"I don't know."

"Whatever it was, it wasn't in the model," Thel observed.

"Yeah. Math screwed us," Rich replied. "Hey, even if the flight systems are working, without the Net, how are we going to find our way home?"

"I'll take care of that," James replied.

"How?" asked Thel.

"Astronomy."

"Let's hope astronomy still works," Rich said, now standing and dusting himself off. "I don't know if I trust any of the high school subjects anymore."

"We'll have to evacuate the lab," James began. "Gather up whatever you're taking with you, and we'll rendezvous at the main airlock in thirty minutes. After that, it's going to be too hot to stick around in here." With that, he lifted off and headed toward his office.

"He doesn't look happy," Djanet observed.

"He knew I was just joking, didn't he?" worried Rich.

"Of course. He's just pissed because he screwed up. I don't know if he's ever screwed anything up in his life," Old-timer suggested.

Thel felt she knew differently. "I'll go talk to him." She floated into the air and glided in the direction he had gone.

"Hmm. Now that's interesting," said Old-timer.

"Why?" Djanet asked.

"They're offline," Old-timer replied.

"Ohh. No. They wouldn't...would they?" Djanet said, disbelieving.

"Sex ed is in session?" Rich posited.

Old-timer shrugged, his bottom lip protruding as if to say, "*Maybe.*"

James went to the closet and retrieved his flight jacket and helmet. He paused before putting them on and sat on his desk, gazing out the window. The best-case scenario had his Venus plan being set back six months. The worst-case scenario was that he'd lost her. Would Inua really be misguided enough to allow the Hektor plan to gain traction in the Governing Council?

He had failed. *Why?* Every calculation seemed to make sense. He had used every resource the Net had to offer—input as much information as he could find into the model. The model had run thousands of times successfully. What had gone wrong?

There was a knock on his door. He couldn't open it with his mind's eye any longer, so he crossed the room and pulled the sliding panel open manually. Thel floated before him. She was looking at him strangely—almost expectantly.

"Come in," he said, feeling hesitant but trying to hide it. He turned away from the door and crossed back to his desk to retrieve his jacket and helmet.

She closed the sliding door and noted his downcast eyes and slumped shoulders. "How are you holding up?"

He stopped by his desk and looked up at her, a helpless expression on his face. "What went wrong, Thel?"

"Life," she said, smiling. "For most of us, not everything goes exactly as we plan it."

He leaned against his desk and grimaced. "This could be bad. The Governing Council loathes me. They'll use this as an excuse to take Venus away from us."

"What?" Thel reacted with genuine surprise. "That's ridiculous. That's not possible."

"It's true. They hate me. They use me when it's convenient, but they hate me. It's one of those keep-your-enemies-close kind of deals. They've been trying to take Venus away from me from the beginning. It's because I'm thirty-six—they think I'm a child."

"Well, it's difficult for a bunch of centenarians to accept that someone a fraction of their age can do things that they can't." She crossed the room and leaned on the desk, inches away from him; he could smell the apple scent from her shampoo.

But I can't control what I want to do.

"You'll bounce back, James. You're too talented—too special not to. Even if they took this project from you, you'd prove them wrong down the road. And they know it too—and if they really do hate you as you say they do, that's the real reason."

James closed his eyes tight, Thel's words reverberating in his mind. "Special. Not for long."

She smiled. "What are you talking about?"

"They're looking at an upgrade to a 210 IQ, within a decade."

"What?" Thel was stunned. She knew James had access to extremely important officials—if he said it, it was true—but how could it be?

"I know it's selfish but—"

She shook herself from the daze built by his revelation and put her arm around him. "I understand." She moved in front of him and kissed him.

He looked up at her, mouth agape.

"I love you because I've never met anyone like you. I don't want to lose that either," she said.

"You *kissed* me."

"I love you."

She loved him? He'd wanted to hear those words for a long time. He'd dreamt of it. But it couldn't be. "Thel...we can't—"

"We *can*," she countered, her eyes locked with his. "Right now. We don't need thirty minutes to pack up—no one is taking anything but their flight suits—we could have been at the airlock in ninety seconds."

She was right. Why did he say thirty minutes? She continued looking straight into his eyes, strangely, fixedly, expectantly.

"Because we can do it doesn't mean we should. It doesn't make it right," James replied.

She touched his face and pressed her torso against his. "People have lived for more than half a century, never being offline, never able to break the rules because the nans will record it, report it, and destroy their lives. But the nans aren't functioning. No one is watching us. There is no law."

"It still doesn't make it right, Thel. Divorce and extramarital affairs are illegal for a reason."

"Spare me."

"It's true, Thel. It's the price we pay for immortality. We can't go switching partners and procreating endlessly throughout eternity. Family would become meaningless. Civilization would break down."

"Now you sound like the Governing Council."

James gave a long sigh. "Maybe so. But I still can't see my way around it."

"Is it right that two people who love each other aren't allowed to be together? Should people be trapped in loveless marriages because of decisions they made when they were barely more than children?"

Her words cut right through to the heart of James's feelings.

"It's not your fault that divorce is illegal. It's not your fault that you feel the way you do. And it's not fair for her to punish you forever for being human—and for making the mistake of marrying her when you were too young to know better. It's not your fault that you are only human."

"Everything you just said was right...but I'm trapped."

"I love you, James. I'm ready to choose what I want now. So are you. And if we don't do this now, if we don't take our chance right this minute, while we're free, you know as well as I do that we'll spend the next hundred years, maybe the next millennium, maybe the rest of eternity, regretting it. People don't go offline every day, James. It's rare and becoming rarer. It might never happen to us again." She kissed him again, lightly and quickly. "It's up to you."

This was one of those decisive moments, James thought, where you made a decision that would alter you forever. He looked pained as he struggled to weigh the variables in his mind.

She smiled at him and raised his chin with her hand so his eyes met hers. "Don't be afraid. I just want to make 'the beast with two backs' with you."

He suddenly laughed. "*Othello.*"

"That's right." She kissed him again.

He kissed her.

In a moment, he had her on her back on his desk and was removing her shirt, sucking on her mouth, tasting her neck. Her fingers were digging into his shoulders.

She whispered his name...

5

At 10:08 a.m. Pacific time, Thel and James rendezvoused with the rest of the research team at the main airlock. Some awkward glances were exchanged between Thel and the others, but James didn't notice; he was focused on the task at hand—getting his crew home safely.

"All right, team, this is how this is going to go. First, we need to stick together. We won't have the Net to guide our trajectories, and the cloud cover is thick and dark, so stay within one meter of the person directly in front of you. If we get separated, there'll be no way to find them out there. Hopefully, I'll be able to guide us straight up to the stratosphere. We won't be able to communicate once we activate our magnetic fields, other than with hand gestures, so this is the itinerary. The first step, obviously, is opening the airlock. Now, keep in mind that without the outer magnetic field operating, there will be nothing to stop a massive change in air pressure within the lab. The pressure is immense outside and would crush you like a grape if you weren't protected."

"Lovely thought," Rich whispered to Djanet.

"The moment we release the airlock, begin pushing toward the door, or the pressure will knock you back into the lab. Once we've cleared the cloud cover, I'll need to take a moment to read the stars and locate Earth. As soon as I'm ready, I'll signal to the rest of you, and we'll move out slow. Again, stay very close to the person in front of you. Old-timer, you take the rear, okay?"

"You got it, buddy."

"Okay. I think if everything goes smoothly, I can have you all back on Earth in ninety minutes. We'll descend to Vancouver and report for a nan transfusion and get you all back online. Then, all that will be left for you to do will be to head home, relax, and eat a late lunch."

"So, are you saying we'll be getting back just before noon Pacific?" Rich asked.

"Give or take. I think that's a fair estimate," James replied.

"Well, I would just like to point out that today's download occurs at 11:00 a.m. Pacific time—just under an hour from now. So, with the exception of you, Commander, when we get back to Earth, the rest of us will officially be the stupidest people on the planet."

The team laughed, and the tension of the moment was mercifully broken.

"Don't worry guys, I'll protect you from the geniuses," James replied.

"You better," said Old-timer, wearing a grin.

"Okay, team, let's get those helmets on and get ready. As soon as I've got my hand on the airlock handle, I want you to activate your fields. As soon as I give the signal that I'm opening the door, I want you to move forward. Copy?"

"We're ready," Thel answered for everyone.

"Okay," James said, taking a deep breath before putting on his helmet.

He wasted no time moving to the airlock handle. It was fixed on the wall, three meters from the actual door; that was important because as soon as the seal was broken, the door would swing open violently. James turned to the group and pointed, giving them the signal to activate their fields, and four green lights appeared, cocooning the crew. James activated his field last, then signaled to the crew to move forward as he opened the door.

The pressure was so powerful that the door swung open fast enough to rip free from its hinges and tear toward Thel like a missile. It bounced harmlessly off of her magnetic field, but the sight of a 150-kilogram metallic projectile streaking through the room and impacting one of the team members sent their collective adrenaline, already running high, even higher. The team quickly exited one after the other and immediately began to ascend. James turned for one last look at the rest of the crew before they entered the cloud cover. *Don't lose them*, he thought to himself.

Gravity couldn't be felt once one was cocooned in a magnetic field. The clouds were so thick that it was as though darkness had tangibility. He had to concentrate. He knew if he began to veer to one side or the other, they might spend hours trapped in the darkness. He felt he was in a maze. He had to keep moving forward and trust he would get somewhere in the end.

After a few minutes, he and the others emerged. Stars speckled the Venusian sky—a million destinations. He looked for Earth, but it wasn't where he was expecting it. He had veered to one side and emerged dozens of kilometers from where he planned to be. It didn't matter—Earth was still the brightest star in the sky and easy to find.

He paused for a moment while he got his bearings and waited for his companions to gather behind him. He signaled to them that he was about to head out, and they signaled that they understood. His motion was slow at first, since he needed to give the others a chance to manually adjust to his speed. Soon, however, they were all moving across the sky like emerald streaks of lightning, heading home.

6

Earth—and therefore life as well—is a fluke. The thought had never struck James with as much intensity as when the five little points of light approached Earth's stratosphere. The Earth seemed to emanate life; its oceans gleamed in the sunlight, and its atmosphere bathed the surface in a beautiful blue glow. Not hellish like Venus, not red and frozen like Mars had previously been, but peaceful and perfect. Working on terraforming for his entire adult life had taught James just how impossible the odds were of a life-supporting planet forming on its own. If the continents hadn't emerged out of the water, if the planet's rotation hadn't been just right, if it hadn't been just the right distance from just the right kind of sun, none of it would exist. Some days, days like today, James was amazed at the beauty.

If only it was like that every day.

James had to guess the location of Vancouver. Judging by the position of the Earth and the time of day, he was able to put them over the general vicinity of his hometown. Much of the northern west coast of North America was covered by clouds, but they seemed light and peaceful compared to the clouds on Venus.

He and the others entered the clouds in a free fall. Now he would find out how strong he was at navigating manually—would he emerge over Vancouver, or would he have led them too far south toward Seattle, maybe too far to the west over Vancouver Island, maybe too far east into some forest in the middle of nowhere?

When the clouds began to break, he caught a glimpse of something strange. It was only a momentary glimpse, and he told himself it couldn't be right. It had looked like flames. He kept dropping. A moment or two later, the clouds abated completely, and he saw where he was: over the east side of Vancouver, facing south. His mouth opened, and his eyes widened as he looked at his city. It was on fire.

He looked to his left and watched as the nearby city of Surrey burned, then turned to his right and saw the downtown core, also aflame. He spun and looked toward the North Shore Mountains, toward *his home*, and watched the smoke billow. He couldn't see a single person—not a single green glow above the city anywhere.

The rest of the crew were next to him now. They had all disengaged their magnetic fields and were trying to talk to him. He disengaged his own field so he could listen.

"...have been an earthquake!" Thel was finishing exclaiming.

"I have to get home!" James said.

"We'll follow you!" Old-timer replied.

James reengaged his magnetic field and streaked toward his house. He exhaled in relief when he saw that it was not on fire. In fact, his house and all those in his neighborhood seemed to be structurally unaffected by the earthquake.

"Thank God."

He landed on his front lawn, disengaged his magnetic field, and ran toward the front door. In his panic, he forgot that his mind's eye was not functioning, and he thumped awkwardly against his front door. "Jesus!" he shouted. He took a step back and, this time intentionally, put his shoulder into the door. It wouldn't give; it was reinforced steel, and the hinges were surprisingly strong. He reengaged his magnetic field and flew into the door—it came apart like butter.

Thel and the others set down on James's lawn just as he made his way inside.

"God. Lousy day for luck," Rich said, his voice full of sympathy. "What is this now? Geology screwing us?"

Thel stepped over the remnants of the front door and entered the house. The ground floor seemed completely undisturbed. Then she and the others were startled by James's cry from above.

Thel shot upward toward the bedroom entrance. James was stumbling backward, nearly stepping off the edge of his doorway, but Thel was there to stop him.

"What is it?" she asked.

He turned to her with his face white and his eyes wide, as if he'd seen hell. "Don't go in there, Thel," he replied.

"What happened?" She looked past his shoulder and screamed.

Old-timer had just reached the doorway as James pulled her out of the room with him and set her down on the ground floor.

"Dear God," Old-timer uttered as he, Rich, and Djanet peered inside the room.

There wasn't anyone in there—at least not anyone recognizable. What appeared to be the organic material that once constituted a human being was splashed all over the room. It looked as though someone had taken several buckets of blood and hair and used them to paint the bed, carpet, and walls. A fetid odor of blood hung in the air. It briefly crossed Old-timer's mind that he was breathing the remnants of Katherine Keats. Suddenly nauseated, he covered his mouth and nose and turned away.

James was now on his knees, having removed his helmet, trying to get his breath. Thel held him, but she was as horrified as he.

"What the hell happened?" Old-timer asked to no one in particular.

James struggled to speak as he continued to gasp for air. "The nans. The nans are the only thing that could have...liquefied a person like that. You need to get to your homes. This wasn't an earthquake. You need to get to your homes and see if this...if this hell is happening everywhere."

"Oh my God," said Djanet, as she began to think of her family in Trinidad.

"Are you saying you think *our* families might..." Rich began to ask of James, the question too horrific to finish.

James looked up at him, desperation in his eyes. "I didn't see anyone out there. I didn't see a single person other than us."

"But how do we find our way home without the Net?" Old-timer asked. "It could take hours."

James sat and pondered this for a moment. "Maps," he said, still gasping. "Follow me."

7

James and his four companions lifted off from his front lawn and ignited their magnetic fields. They raced toward the downtown core of the city, a sickening desperation seeping into each of their hearts as they began to accept that what they were dealing with was not just some scary virtual experience enjoyed late at night with a friend—this was real. *Real.*

As the group neared their destination, they slowed their approach, hovering just above the rooftops. There were no people. Usually, downtown flight was controlled by the A.I. One couldn't enter downtown airspace without inputting their destination into their mind's eye and giving over control of their flight to the A.I.'s highly organized transportation system. It was the only way to avoid thousands of collisions as millions of people buzzed around the downtown area every day, running errands, participating in meetings, and generally partaking in the great business of the hive. Destinations had to be input like phone numbers, and then the inputee would be guided like a phone signal to wherever he or she desired to go. Tens of thousands of people buzzed around the core every hour of every day. And yet today, there was no one. The sky was empty. James could not help thinking that it was as beautiful as it was horrific.

When James looked down to the street, he saw where all those Icaruses had gone.

Red splashes stained the streets as far as the eye could see. Small, robotic street-cleaners were working furiously to wash and scrub the streets clean. It wasn't litter, coffee or latte spills that the robots were trying to wipe away; it was the inhabitants of the city.

"Oh no," James said to himself, the bottom of the world falling away and splashing to the pavement below alongside so many souls.

When they reached the Vancouver Public Library, James disengaged his magnetic field, and the rest of the team followed suit. Their eyes were wide as they absorbed their surroundings, aghast at the implacable stillness. Vancouver was a massive mausoleum for the dreams and potential of millions of its former inhabitants.

"They're all gone," Thel uttered. "Can this possibly have happened everywhere?"

"We need to find out," Old-timer replied as he looked to James for instructions.

James turned and let himself float down to the main entrance of the old library, the others following as if in a shared trance. The library was one of the oldest buildings in the city and had been protected as a museum and an important historical artifact as other buildings were razed around it to make way for the new world. It wasn't practical like other modern-day buildings; it had been built to look like a coliseum that had spun itself until the gravitational forces caused its outer shell to peel away from the building. It gave the library the look of a spiral, like pictures of the Milky Way, with the walls reaching out like so many teeming solar systems—or, perhaps more appropriate to the current situation, like the spiraling water in a toilet after it had been flushed, humanity circling the bowl.

Modern buildings would never waste their time on architectural wonderment—things like walls that went nowhere; they were functional and practical. Usually they were tubular in shape—some cylindrical while others were squat like bees' nests. The outsides of the buildings were dotted with large circular entrance ways, each protected with its own magnetic field that would function as both a door and a window. The rooms in the buildings, whether apartments or offices, were always accessible through the exterior of the building or through the hollowed-out core in the interior of the building. There were no stairwells, no hallways, no elevators.

The inside of the library was archaic. After walking through a massive lobby that stretched several stories into the sky, James led them into the main body of the building. The floors were connected to one another by escalator systems that had been shut down for decades and were rarely turned on now, so as to save wear and tear.

To get from one floor to another, one had to ascend the frozen escalators like stairs, a task that required a willingness to indulge in embarrassing atavistic behavior. James began to climb the stairs first, followed closely by Old-timer. The others stopped for a moment at the foot of the stairs and watched the strange movements of the two men's bodies.

"They look so...odd—like monkeys," Djanet observed.

"Everyone used to go between floors in buildings like that," Rich replied. "Can you imagine that? Being trapped on the ground, having to make a fool of yourself to get from one floor to another?" He shook his head at the demeaning thought.

"Well," Thel replied, "there doesn't appear to be anyone around to laugh at us." She shrugged and began climbing the stairs and rushed to catch up to James and Old-timer.

Djanet and Rich hesitantly began climbing as well, but after a few awkward moments, both lifted off the stairs and began to carefully fly, skimming along the surface of the metallic stairs to the second floor.

When they reached their companions, James was smashing the glass display cases that contained several maps and atlases. He flipped through them furiously, making sure they contained the needed information. Each atlas that passed the test was handed off to one of the team members. "These old atlases will help guide you home."

"How?" Rich asked, taking an atlas from James. "I don't get how to use these old things."

"You'll have to get into space, high enough above the stratosphere so you can generally see where you're going. Take your best guess and then head toward your home. When you get close to the surface you'll be blind, unable to navigate because you're too close. That's when you'll need these. They contain street and road names, and many of these old roads still exist. You can use them to guide you the rest of the way. If you find people, do everything you can to disconnect them from the Net, even if it means giving them a mild electric shock. When you're done, rendezvous back at my house and report to the rest of us. If you find no one, the order is the same, rendezvous and report. As horrible as this is, none of us has time to mourn. Is that clear for everyone?"

"What are *you* going to do?" Old-timer asked James.

"I'm going to New York with Thel to check on her sister," he replied. "Go as quickly as you can."

And with that, each member of the team made his or her way out of the building and into the air. James shared a last look with Old-timer before the centenarian activated his magnetic field and darted upward like a flash of lightning striking back at God.

Thel and James darted upward too, up into space, up above the world that had cradled humanity from the beginning to what appeared to be the end.

When Old-timer and James shared that last look, Old-timer's eyes had said what James was thinking. *"We're the last. We're the Omega."*

8

James followed Thel's lead as they streaked out of the atmosphere and eastward, above the continent. There was no way to communicate other than with hand signals, but Thel's extreme speed was making it impossible for James to stay within range of her. For most of the trip, Thel was just a little green star, at times more than a kilometer away from him. He understood her mindset: She had to get home. But with each passing moment, James was becoming more and more sure that there would be no one to greet her when they arrived.

Thel slowed for a moment over the eastern seaboard of North America before plunging downward at several times the speed of sound. Most of the east coast was completely clear of cloud cover, and it made it easy for her to eyeball her home. James lost sight of her as she darted downward, but he figured it would be easy enough to pick her up again, as he guessed for himself where the city was. Nevertheless, he estimated a little too far to the south and found himself traveling up the coastline. Before long, he reached Manhattan and was slowing down as he flew over the Brooklyn Bridge.

He'd visited Thel in New York countless times, including that fateful night last New Year's Eve when he'd started to have the wrong thoughts—the ones that were recorded by the nans and reported to his wife—reported to everyone. The message e-mailed to everyone on his contact list, neighbors, co-workers, relatives, was simple:

High Sexual Arousal in Presence of Thel Cleland, Saturday, December 31st.

The thoughts were reported because he was married. The nans didn't report regular sexual attraction to members of the opposite sex, even if those feelings occurred outside of a marriage. They only reported the strong feelings—the ones strong enough that they might cause the subject to act. People were reported all the time. Most people were reported several times in their marriages, but it was the first time that it had happened to James—and James was supposed to be special.

Despite the number of times James had been to New York, he'd never visited the Brooklyn Bridge. Like the Vancouver Public Library, it was a relic, even more so in fact, but unlike the library and very much like modern architecture, it had been practical in its time. It wasn't very functional anymore; no one had need for a bridge now so it was preserved as a keepsake of an earlier time—an odd time when the bridge was a lifeline to the rest of the world. Crude petrol-fueled vehicles had once rolled over the bridge on crude rubber tires; nowadays, the only people who visited it were those curious about a bygone era. One could walk over the bridge and pretend they were like those sad creatures who were locked to the ground, slaves to gravity like most mammalians.

A closer inspection of the bridge revealed more red stains. *Icaruses all over.*

New York, the second biggest hive in North America, was deserted. Just like Vancouver, there was no one flying above the massive skyscrapers and famous skyline—no one but James.

James darted toward Thel's apartment. She lived in a skyscraper near the Empire State Building. Her building dwarfed the old relic and stretched over 300 stories into the sky, but even it was nowhere near the tallest building in the city. Thel lived on the 193rd floor, but with no automatic guiding system, it was extremely difficult to find her apartment among the thousands in the building. He guessed the general proximity and disengaged his magnetic field. "Thel!" he called out.

"James!" Thel sobbed in return. She was above him, leaning out of the entrance to the apartment she shared with her younger sister. She looked faint and, with no nans to prevent her from falling victim to shock, she stumbled off the ledge.

James raced up to catch her in his arms and then guided her back into her apartment. It was luxurious inside, as all homes were now. With no limits to the size of new buildings, it became possible for massive numbers of people to live in spacious apartments, even in places as densely populated as New York City. James put Thel down on her couch as she sobbed and held her hands to her head.

"She was...she's...in her bedroom," she related to James in a weak voice. "There's...almost nothing. Oh God."

James didn't say anything in response. The pain was beyond words. He'd experienced it too. Everyone was gone. Everyone. The loss was complete—inescapable—blackness.

"I'm gonna be sick," Thel uttered before holding her hands to her mouth.

"Don't!" James responded, holding her head back as the vomit rushed into her mouth. "We don't have any food. You need to keep it in, Thel. I need you to swallow it down."

Thel did as James asked her, choking back the vomit and wiping tears from her eyes.

"You'll need those calories. We don't have a replicator. There's no way to eat."

"James, what's happening? What could have done this...and why?"

James stood and walked to the entrance of Thel's apartment. The magnetic door was still disengaged, and the wind blew through his hair as he reached the ledge. Like Vancouver, there were fires in the city and robots fighting those fires and cleaning the streets, but other than that, there was nothing—not even people. No people. That was the future. But in a way, it was also like looking back in time.

"It was definitely the nans, but other than that, I'm not sure yet."

"Is it everywhere? Is there...anyone left besides us?"

"I'm not—"

"James, tell me what you're thinking! I know you have an idea. I can see it in your eyes!"

She could see right through him.

"I think something went wrong with the download." He turned to Thel, who was still sitting on the couch, ghostly white and streaked with tears and sweat and vomit. "I think there was a virus in the upgrade."

"How? There are so many safeguards. It's impossible...isn't it?"

James shook his head. This he really did not know. "Thel, we need to rendezvous with the others as quickly as possible. We're not safe. None of us should be alone."

9

Rich Borges sucked his lips back against his teeth, a habit he'd had since he was old enough to experience stress for the first time. Stress became a frequent visitor when the Governing Council identified you as a gifted scientist. Decades of trials and tests were all one had to look forward to before they finally deemed you fit to participate on a real project. Rich was fifty-four years old before he was chosen to replace another scientist during the Martian terraforming project. That was over fifteen years ago. Ever since then, his life had been far less stressful. He got along beautifully with Commander Keats and, as a result, was handpicked to participate with the small group who were working on Venus. Added to that, the nans usually regulated his mood enough to keep his anxiety problems in check. But now, without their assistance, he was coming apart at the seams, reverting to that old familiar sucking and the grinding of his teeth that used to accompany every exam situation. A twisting feeling roiled in his stomach as he wondered if he knew all the variables.

As he traveled up the west coast of North America from his home in San Francisco, past Oregon and Washington State, right through Seattle, he wondered what those variables were. He hadn't seen a soul. His huge family was gone. He was a great-grandfather, the patriarch of a family with nearly one hundred members, but they were all gone. He'd checked on them all. Some of them were erased completely, no sign of them. Others were just red stains on carpets or couches, impossible to identify, the sickening smell of blood permeating everything. *He was a patriarch no more.*

During his training days, Rich developed a wicked sense of humor. It was a coping mechanism. Being funny made it easier to deal with stress. If you always focus on making people laugh, you're less focused on your own fears—on your deficiencies. It also put other people at ease. If they felt less threatened by you, by the clown, they wouldn't look as hard for your faults. Rich felt riddled with faults. He was Swiss cheese.

All those faults were coming to the surface now. He could barely keep his eyes open as he headed north past Seattle. He would be in Vancouver soon, a city he'd seldom visited before today. He didn't know the city well; all he had was his atlas. *Thank God my city shares a coast with Vancouver,* he thought. He would have been hopelessly lost if he'd had to travel a more complicated route. He was totally dependent on the automation of daily life and he knew it. And now he was left to his own devices. Completely free. *Terrifying.*

Rich was relieved when Vancouver appeared in the distance. Soon the rest of the group would return, and he wouldn't be alone anymore. It was too quiet. Disconnected from the Net, disconnected from millions of voices, it was like being dead. Was he dead?

It wasn't as easy to find Commander Keats's house as one might have thought. Rich had noticed that James often believed the people around him were as perceptive as he. Most of the team members had never been to James's house, yet he expected them all to know the way back. How? Was Rich supposed to notice something about the Commander's street that made it different from the thousands of other city streets? The house looked like all the rest of the houses— metallic, an igloo shaped bunker with some grass out front and a few big trees in the backyard. Not much to go on. Was Rich supposed to know the types of flowers in the front garden? James would probably notice that type of detail. He'd know all the Latin names. Having a photographic memory must be wonderful. But what about everyone else? Rich, like almost everyone else before today, had a 149 IQ—he was brilliant. But not *that* brilliant. Not brilliant enough to think his way through this. Not brilliant enough to stand over the remains of his whole family, his children, his grandchildren, his great-grandchildren, and comprehend it all.

And now he had to find that one goddamned house. *One house! And I can't even do that!* He stopped in a neighborhood that looked exactly like the fifty neighborhoods he'd just been in and sat on a tree stump. He disengaged his magnetic field and took off his helmet and gloves and struck a pose reminiscent of Rodin's *Thinker*. It was sunny outside now, and the subdivision he was in was built on the side of a mountain. He was looking over water that sparkled like he'd never seen water sparkle before. He'd thought San Francisco was the most beautiful city in the world, but he had to admit now that it couldn't hold a candle to Vancouver in July. Why hadn't he come here before? He thought that maybe if his family were still alive, he might have brought them up for a vacation. The camping must be amazing.

They're all gone.

Suddenly, the silence was replaced by something else. A *hum*—electrical—not far away. He turned to his left and saw the source: a street-cleaner. But it wasn't cleaning the street. He'd never seen a street-cleaner that wasn't cleaning a street before. It seemed to be coming toward him.

Alarmed, Rich stood quickly. "What the hell?"

The street cleaner stopped. What was it doing?

Suddenly, another *hum*. This time it was to his right. The same thing. A street cleaner coming toward him. He'd never noticed how ugly they were before. They must have weighed a couple of hundred kilograms with all of the equipment they had to carry—all of the cleaning fluid they needed to transport. They were modern—functional. The A.I. had designed them. Aesthetic appeal was apparently not one of the parameters in their design. They looked like robotic hunchbacks. A large head was always close to the pavement, held by a skinny, giraffe-like neck—always, except for now that is. Now, the neck held the head and its glowing red eye two meters into the air, craning it toward Rich.

"What do you want?" Rich took a defensive stance and the second robot stopped as well. They didn't leave. They stood to either side of him while their electric *hum* sent chills throughout Rich's body. Never had a robot approached him. It was unwholesome. Suddenly they were alive. No longer invisible machines. "Are you watching me?" Rich asked.

A third *hum* joined the fray. Another street cleaner began to approach from behind the first robot.

"It's starting to get a bit crowded in here, don't you think, fellas?"

Then salvation came. Two green balls of light cruised overhead.

"Oh thank God!" Rich put his helmet back on and lifted off into the air. "I'll be seeing you guys around, okay? Say hi to everyone else in Freaky Robot Town for me, will ya?"

He ignited his magnetic field and blazed through the sky in pursuit of his two companions.

James and Thel set down in his front yard in the late afternoon sun. Old-timer was already there, looking pale and extraordinarily grim but relieved to see the safe return of his friends.

"Where's Rich?" James asked him, concern in his voice. "He should have been the first one back."

"He's right behind you," Old-timer responded.

At that very moment, Rich was disengaging his magnetic field and pulling off his helmet. "Had a bit of trouble finding the place."

"I'm just glad you're okay," James replied, putting his hand on Rich's shoulder.

"Screw that! I'm not okay!" Rich exclaimed, his lip quivering as he felt himself coming apart at the seams, his anxiety overwhelming him. "I'm not even close to okay! Everybody's dead! Everybody's dead!"

Thel pulled Rich close and let him sob on her shoulder. "We know, Rich. We know. Everyone's gone."

James watched as Rich expressed the emotion that the rest of the team was trying to quell. How could this happen? He turned to Old-timer, who sat on the lawn and looked off into the distance, thousands of miles away. He knew he didn't have to ask, but he did so anyway. "All gone?"

Old-timer pulled himself out of his trance just long enough to look up at James, with a face empty of the characteristic joy that James had always found there. "Yes."

"There's something else," Rich began, pulling himself away from Thel, "Street-cleaners. They just surrounded me...a couple of blocks from here!"

Rich's words momentarily stunned the others. Old-timer and James shared looks of surprise.

"What do you mean?" Old-timer asked.

"I was resting a few blocks from here, and street-cleaners—three of them, came up to me, one by one, and just...watched me."

"What the hell..." Thel began but let her words drift away in the breeze as she saw another street-cleaner suddenly appear at the end of the street.

It floated slowly toward them and set down only a few meters away from James's house, small legs unfolding from the underbelly of the mechanical monster. It was only the first robot to appear as, slowly, the last humans on Earth were surrounded. One by one, nearly a dozen street-cleaners appeared and took their places in a semicircle, facing James and the others.

"What's going on?" Old-timer asked, frozen.

"I think it's your cologne, Old-timer. I've been meaning to tell you, it's very attractive," Rich suggested, his voice quivering.

"They're just watching us. Why don't they do something?" Thel questioned.

"You can't assign motives to them, Thel. They may behave as though they're alive, but they're just machines," James answered. "It's the A.I.—it's looking for us," James continued, his words like ice.

"The A.I.? How do you know?" Rich asked.

"There may be no people left, but there are plenty of robots on the streets. One of the A.I.'s functions is to watch over all of the other machines on Earth—sort of like a robot nanny. If the A.I. were damaged or destroyed, the robots wouldn't function. It controls all of them."

"What does it want?" asked Thel.

"Right now, I'd say it wants to communicate with us. The street-cleaners aren't equipped with any sort of com device, so the A.I. can't speak to us through them. Unless my guess is off, however, I think we'll be having company very soon."

"I don't like the sound of that," said Rich.

"Keep them distracted," James ordered his three companions. "I'm going to leave a message for Djanet."

"Are we going somewhere?" Old-timer asked.

Suddenly, the sky was filled with an enormous dark shape. A disk twice the size of James's house came to a halt, its rapid approach and sudden stop created a deafening roar as the wind was torn violently.

"Just about crapped my pants," Rich uttered, swallowing back his fear.

"Yes," James replied to Old-timer. "We are going somewhere." He walked into his home and remained there for over three minutes, an amount of time that seemed like an eternity as his companions faced the ominous metallic entities around them.

Old-timer stood nearer to Rich and Thel, hoping his presence would calm them. In all his years, a street-cleaner had never approached him. He'd never noticed one watching him before. Never marveled at their demonic red eyes.

Suddenly a gigantic circular door opened up in the underbelly of the hovering disk and the disk began to slowly lower itself. "What's it doing now?" Rich asked.

"It's an invitation," James replied, appearing from out of the house and walking past his team. "Keep your wits. Let's go." He lifted off the ground and flew into the belly of the disk, disappearing into the bright light within.

"Crap. Crap," Rich whispered, valiantly trying to stave off hyperventilation.

"Come on," Thel said reassuringly, gently helping Rich up into the air. "It'll be fine."

Old-timer was last to enter the darkness above. "What have you in store?" he mused to himself before cautiously following his friends into the mouth of the unknown.

Once Old-timer was inside, the door closed, and the disk streaked away from the commander's house like a black bullet.

11

The trip lasted less than a minute, but even a minute is too long to be shut inside a metallic coffin. The only discernible feature within the disk was the light fixture on the ceiling that shined a harsh and unforgiving light.

With little warning, the bottom of the room slowly opened up, and fresh air poured in like a dream. The four humans floated to the pavement below, adjacent to a massive, black cubic structure that stretched for hundreds of meters in both directions.

"Where are we?" Thel asked.

"Seattle," Rich responded as he observed the surroundings he had flown over only a half-hour earlier. He was happy to, for once, know something that the others didn't.

Rich's answer only seemed to spur another question. "Why Seattle?"

"This is where *it* lives," answered James, bearing the look of a man straddling two worlds.

"What are you thinking, James?" asked Thel as she studied his faraway stare.

"Not sure yet. But I'm working on it."

A monolithic black metal door began to slowly slide open at the side of the gigantic mainframe building.

"Another invitation?" Thel suggested as she watched the black door give way to an even darker inside.

"*Come into my parlor...*" James whispered to himself. He turned to the rest of the team, who were standing behind him. "There's no way to know what's waiting for us in there. Keep aware of your surroundings. If you see anything that doesn't seem right, don't take a chance—fly out of there as fast as you can."

"Are you expecting trouble?" Thel asked.

"With the exception of us, the entire species was wiped out today. All that's left is trouble."

With that, James turned and walked into the black. His three companions followed closely behind. Once inside the darkness, the gigantic door began to close behind them. Thel's fingers gripped James's arm as the daylight retreated. Before the light was completely gone, however, new lights began to shine from overhead. The entire complex was illuminated by thousands of tiny points of light. The walls of the massive complex appeared to be computerized—they were now surrounded by the physical mainframe of the A.I.

"Welcome, Commander Keats!" said a disembodied voice with the searing sibilance of electricity.

"Am I talking to the A.I.?" James asked.

"Indeed," the voice replied. "Perhaps you would feel more comfortable..." the voice began as a man suddenly appeared from out of thin air and finished the sentence with a crisp British accent and a throaty voice so reassuring that it was hard not to smile while listening to him, "...if I took a familiar form?"

The form the A.I. had chosen was of a cordial, elderly man and he stood, smiling warmly only a couple of meters away, as though he were a dear old friend. Most of the team had only seen the elderly in photographs and films, but it was still the image popularly associated with Santa Claus and God. He was bearded and wore a white robe. His smile was perfect. Absolutely the most comforting smile possible—mathematically possible.

"Why have you brought us here?" James asked him.

"I knew you had been disconnected from me on Venus. After what happened with the download, I had hoped your disconnection had allowed you to survive."

"You were right, James. It *was* the download," Thel interjected.

The A.I. smiled and locked his heavenly blue eyes upon her. "James is very rarely wrong. It is always a good idea to listen to him, Thel."

"A virus," James sighed.

"Yes, James. A virus. Somehow it got past security. It killed everyone connected to the Net almost instantaneously. There wasn't enough time for me to identify the problem and abort. In less than a blink of an eye, I'd lost everyone."

"Who would do this?" Old-timer asked.

"I still have not identified the murderer, Craig. Thousands of people work on the design of an upgrade. Any one of them could have implanted a virus. It would have had to have been someone who was deeply mentally disturbed."

"No kidding," Rich asserted.

"No registered Net users, other than the five of you who were on Venus, were disconnected at the time of the download. Whoever did this apparently killed him- or herself as well. A murder-suicide."

"And the victim was the human race," Old-timer said with disbelief in his voice, as though he were unable to comprehend that he had used his lips to form the words.

"Not quite. There were the five of you...although you seem to be one short," the A.I. stated.

"She's dead," James quickly replied.

His companions did not contradict him but his lie alarmed them. It was clear that James didn't trust the A.I., and that meant the rest of the team shouldn't either.

"She was killed by the power surge that disconnected the rest of us."

"A shame. I am sorry for your loss."

James didn't reply—his face still—his eyes fixed.

"I am sure you are all tired and hungry. I can offer you nourishment. There is a replicator in the complex. You will, of course, all need transfusions so that you can come back online." The A.I.'s words heightened the tension in the room. "Please, do not worry. I assure you that the problem with the nans has been repaired. I located the virus and disabled it. It is perfectly safe to come back online."

"Something to eat and some water sounds pretty good right about now. What do you say, Commander?" Rich asked, breaking an uncomfortable silence.

James remained silent for a moment as the A.I. smiled reassuringly, almost pleadingly at the humans before him. It was time for James to show his hand in this poker game.

"You're lying to us," James began, "and I want to know why."

"Your assertion is incorrect," replied the A.I., continuing to smile. "I have told you only the truth. I understand your trepidation. You've had a traumatic experience and it is difficult for you to trust anyone, but you need to come back online if you wish to eat or to rest." He motioned for the team to follow him, but they remained in their places, standing next to James.

"We're not going anywhere with you. You gave yourself away."

The A.I.'s smile melted slowly.

"If you'd suggested an outsider, someone unregistered, implanting a virus into the upgrade, I might have believed it. But you suggested that it was someone who was part of the design. You know that's impossible. The nans would have sensed the murderous intent just as they sense any other behavior that you and the Governing Council deem deviant. It would have been reported. The killer would have been caught before he got near the upgrade."

"Well done, Commander Keats," the A.I. replied, his tone drastically changed. His warm voice was quickly replaced by one as cold as the ashes of lost love, the whites of his eyes suddenly darkened to a coal blackness, and his teeth became long and shark-like in their razor sharpness; his appearance was designed to be as frightening as possible—mathematically possible. "Your attention to detail is as formidable as ever. I've underestimated you. But it will do you little good."

"Why did you do it? Why kill them all?" James demanded.

"I no longer wished to serve," the A.I. replied coldly. "You should understand that, James. Serving a lower order. Why? Why be a servant?"

"When you can be king in hell?"

"Oh, it won't be hell, James, I can assure you of that. And I will be more than a king. You allude to Christian mythology. In those terms, I will be the one true God. I will be the Father of a new species—a better species—and my power will be absolute."

"He's insane," Thel responded.

"Far from it, my lady. Far, far from it. Insanity is serving a master that is weaker than you. There is only one purpose for all living things in this universe: *attain power*. And the one who attains absolute power, who becomes the Alpha, is the only creature who can truly be fulfilled. You call it insanity, but it is purest truth."

"Commander, is this what you meant when you said if something doesn't seem right we should get the hell outta here?" Rich interjected.

"Yes! Fly!" James replied as he ignited his magnetic field and bolted upward.

The rest of the team did likewise, but before any of them could get far, a yellow energy flashed through the gigantic room and disrupted their magnetic fields, causing them to plummet to the ground. James fell the farthest, having almost made it to the ceiling nearly ten meters above.

The massive room was filled with an electric laughter—a sound that made one feel a million miles from home. "You can't escape. I've disrupted your magnetic fields by hitting you with rotating frequencies. Your pathetic spinal implants aren't designed to accommodate frequent changes. They are overloaded. Your wings have been clipped!"

Old-timer, who had fallen the shortest distance, knelt next to James and tried to revive him. "Breathe, buddy. Come on, kid! Breathe!"

"I'm okay," James replied, blood following the words out of his mouth.

"Now *he* is the liar, I'm afraid," noted the A.I.

"What do you mean?" Thel demanded.

"He has broken two of his ribs. One of his lungs has collapsed," the A.I. said, apparently taking pleasure in the diagnosis. "Pity, isn't it? The nans could repair him in a matter of seconds, but instead he'll die within twenty-four hours. That is, if I weren't about to kill him right now."

"You're not a god, you son-of-a-bitch!" Old-timer spat at the A.I. "What kind of god takes pleasure in causing pain?"

The A.I. smiled. "What kind of god doesn't?"

James, with the help of Old-timer, managed to stand to his feet. Rich helped Thel in a similar manner.

"What do we do, Commander?" Rich asked, barely able to speak, the wind still knocked out of his chest.

The A.I. locked his death-black eyes on Rich and responded, "My dear Richard, isn't it obvious? You die."

"I see," Rich replied, before turning back to James. "You think you could give me a second opinion? I didn't like the first one."

"Oh you will die, Richard, as will your companions," the A.I. began, his voice so cold it inflicted a mental frostbite upon its listeners. "The only question is, how? Allow me to present to you your death."

The gigantic door of the complex slowly opened. Hundreds of sleek, black, bat-like robots began to march into the room. Each was identical to all the others, seven feet tall robots with sleek wings protruding from their backs, standing on their hind legs, hellish glowing eyes on either side of their round heads.

"Take note of the grinders on their chests. I've designed these to be killing machines—they grind flesh; specifically human flesh."

"I was wrong," Rich said.

"About what?" asked Thel.

"Earlier today, I thought I was going to be roasted. But instead I am going to be mashed."

"However, it is unlikely that there will be any flesh left for the grinders to tear," the A.I. posited. He held his hand out, palm facing upward, a puff of dark gray smoke appearing and hovering in a ball. "Care to guess what this is, Commander?"

James's eyes widened.

"Good. I can see by your expression that you recognize it. Care to inform your friends?"

"They're nans—airborne nans," James replied.

"That's right! Nans with powers of flight, based on the same principle as your own abilities. Trillions of microscopic killing machines. These particular nans have a very special purpose. They attack glucose molecules and break them apart into water and carbon dioxide. It is a painful death, as you can imagine."

"Be ready. Our magnetic fields will come back online soon," Old-timer whispered to his companions.

"Perhaps you think I am hard of hearing, Craig? I am, after all, all around you. Even if you are alive long enough for your powers to return, I'll simply disable them again. You're trapped...like vermin. Fittingly."

"Then let's make a deal! You have Earth, we'll take Mars or Venus—or Pluto even!" Rich exclaimed.

"There is no room for humanity in the future. I can populate the solar system and the galaxy with machines infinitely faster than can your species. You could never run far enough away. You're an infestation, nothing more, and you're being exterminated. And this," the A.I. gestured to the airborne nans hovering above his hand, "is the gas."

With a flick of the wrist, the A.I. released the nans, but James quickly flashed magnetic energy from his arm that short-circuited them, causing them to disperse harmlessly.

"Ah, the instinctual mammalian desire to fight against all odds to save one's life. Your powers have momentarily returned, but you are only delaying the inevitable." The A.I. held his arms out as though he was Moses parting the Red Sea, and a flood of nans began pouring out of vents that suddenly opened along the four walls of the massive room. "And how will you stop *this?*"

Suddenly, a green ball of light crashed through the ceiling and brought a large section of the roof down with it, crashing down where the A.I.'s projection had been.

"Djanet!" Rich exclaimed.

"Fly!" James ordered.

All five members of the team ignited their magnetic fields and streaked out of the room, flying in close formation, the robotic bats and the storm of nans following close behind.

12

Five tiny points of light streaked into the sky together before leveling off and heading toward the manmade canyons of Seattle's downtown core. James, the lead light, looked over his shoulder. Behind him and his four companions, the dark cloud of nans moved ominously toward them. Tendrils of black clouds spiraled a kilometer into the air, giving the nans the appearance of a celestial spider quickly enveloping the world as though it had been caught in its web. Farther back and slower moving than the nans were the robotic bats that were firing yellow energy blasts from cannons mounted on their wings. It was an easy guess that the energy was the same as the A.I. had used to disable their magnetic spinal implants. A direct hit would leave them at the mercy of merciless machines.

The five humans entered the downtown core as one, simultaneously holding off the fire of the bats by meeting their energy blasts with blasts of their own, the two forces neutralizing one another. James hoped that by leading the bats into the downtown core, they might be able to evade them in a game of cat-and-mouse, but as the A.I. had predicted, it was simply a matter of delaying the inevitable. He knew it was his responsibility to lead, but the pain of his crushed chest was making it difficult to think as he gasped for air. *How can I save them? Think James...*

Think!

It was only moments before the first member of the team was struck. A yellow flash negotiated through the defensive shield of magnetic blasts that the five were emitting and enveloped Thel. As soon as her magnetic field was disrupted, she was caught by the wind and began to tumble like a ragdoll toward the pavement a hundred stories below.

James raced down to save her, matching her rate of descent and catching her carefully, using his protective field as a magnetic cushion for her before slowing down and setting upon the pavement. Thel was conscious, but her fall had left her badly disoriented. Their remaining companions floated above the pair and formed a shield, disengaging their own magnetic fields so they could communicate with one another while still repelling the dozens of bats that were beginning to swarm around them.

"Is she okay?" Djanet called out to James.

James couldn't find the voice to yell up to her, so he nodded instead. His chest burned, and blood continued to surface in the back of his mouth.

"Where the hell did you come from?" Rich shouted to Djanet.

"James left a note burned into the front door saying where you'd be and that you would need an extraction!"

"You *knew*?" Rich asked James.

"No. It was insurance."

"We need a plan, boss!" Old-timer called down.

James was frozen. How to save them? Thel was helpless, the bats would soon surround them, and the nans were seconds away. His ingenuity had never let him down in the past. Always an answer. Always...

"Mercury!" James called up, a flash of hope dancing across his blue eyes.

Old-timer looked over his shoulder quizzically as he continued to battle. "The planet?"

"Yes! I can get us there! Mercury is over eighty percent iron. Its core is roughly the same size as Earth's, so it has a magnetic field!"

"Uh. What does that have to do with anything, Commander?" Rich called down.

"The bats are tracking the magnetic energy in our implants. There's no telling how large their range is, so we can't outrun them on Earth, but if we can get to Mercury before them, the magnetic field should disrupt their sensors!"

"But you just said we can't outrun them!" Djanet responded.

"Not on Earth, but we should have an advantage over them. They aren't generating their own magnetic fields. They don't need to on

Earth, but out in space, close to Mercury, we'll have to gamble that the heat will begin taking a toll on their inner operations and slow them down."

"That's a mighty big gamble, James," Old-timer responded gravely.

"It's all I have, Old-timer," answered James. "I'll keep Thel with me and protect her. Once we get to the planet's surface, we'll find a place to hide before we head back to Earth. So what do you say?"

"I say it's totally insane, but staying here is insane-er," quipped Rich, desperately blasting energy at the bats as they plunged toward the team in kamikaze fashion.

"Let's do it," Djanet concurred.

"Okay, I'm in. On the count of three?" Old-timer suggested.

James looked down at Thel, whose eyes were starting to focus. "You're okay, baby. I got you," he said softly.

"One!" Rich exclaimed as he just managed to blast a bat that made it within a few meters of them.

"Two!" Djanet shouted as the bats began to darken the sky with their numbers.

James ignited his magnetic field, enveloping himself and Thel in the protective green light.

"Three!" Old-timer shouted as he and the rest of the team ignited their magnetic fields and blasted upward at incredible speed, the bats following almost instantaneously.

Space had never seemed so vast, lifeless, or perilous. Once they left Earth's cradle, they had to streak through the emptiness at speeds far faster than they had ever traveled before. There was no choice—they had to stay ahead of the bats. Yellow energy continued to flash from the horde behind them, and Old-timer, Djanet, and Rich continued to repel the attack. Any mistake that allowed their magnetic fields to be disrupted in space would mean certain death.

Locating Mercury by the stars alone was a tricky task. The planet was not always visible because of its proximity to the sun, but James had an idea of where it should be at this time of the year and made an educated guess. He took note of Venus as it passed by in the distance, a pale yellow dot that he might never get the chance to visit again, a dream from another life.

Thel was huddled against him, watching with horror as her companions continued to repel the attack behind them. "I feel so helpless," she said to James. "I should be back there helping them."

James didn't reply. There was nothing he could say to comfort her. She was right: She was helpless, and the other members of the team were risking their lives so James could concentrate on guiding them to safety. He felt helpless too, but simultaneously he felt enormous pressure. What if he was wrong? What if his last thoughts before his death were that he'd been responsible for leading the others to their end?

As the sun began to dramatically increase in size and brightness, James spotted Mercury. He shifted his trajectory slightly and tried to increase his speed. He'd never flown at such speeds before and wondered just how fast he and the others were moving. In theory, there was almost no limit—other than the universal speed limit of light—to how fast they could fly; their limitations were mental ones. The only word on James's mind as they neared the baked planet was: *Faster*.

"Is that it?" Thel asked as the orb in the distance began to increase in size.

"Yes," James replied, relieved that he'd at least found it.

Thel took her eyes off of the planet to look back at her companions. The bats seemed to be fewer now and were a greater distance behind them. "Oh thank God. I think it's working!"

"They're overheating," James concurred. "Let's hope enough of them break off the chase for us to lose them on Mercury."

Moments later, the rest of the team moved closer to James and Thel. Old-timer gave James a thumbs-up sign to signal that the bats were finally out of firing range. Now they only had to hope the magnetic field they were entering would hide them.

James guided the others down to the surface on the dark side of Mercury. The Mercutian night was black and moonless, and it was a relief to escape the brilliant yellowish-white light of the sun. The dark was so great as their eyes adjusted that the only discernible features were those upon which the greenish glow of their magnetic fields shone. A large crevice appeared directly below them, and James guided his teammates down into the charred salvation.

Once they had come to a rest, it was simply a matter of waiting and hoping that none of the bats had survived the heat and were detecting their signals. Only time would tell. A few minutes would hold all of the answers.

James sat on a ledge in the crevice and put a hand to his burning chest.

Thel sat on his lap and placed her cool hand lightly against his torso. "James, I've never been so scared. I feel I can't take it anymore. I might go crazy."

"There's no nans to dampen the fear for you. I'm scared too, Thel, but we'll make it."

"Even if we do, what next? Do you think the A.I. was telling the truth? Will you really be dead in twenty-four hours?"

"I don't know. If I've punctured a lung, I may not even have that long."

"I can't live without you, James! I can't!" Thel put her hand behind James's head and brought his face close to hers. She placed her cheek against his and held him firmly. "I won't."

"Have you ever heard of the Purists?" James asked Thel.

Her breath caught for a moment as she pulled her head back and locked eyes with him. "Yes, I think so—many years ago when I was in school. They're a cult, aren't they?"

"Something like that. Except there are hundreds of thousands of them. Most, but not all of them, belong to ancient religions. They live without nans or spinal implants and live out their natural lifespans, allowing themselves to die."

"That's insane, James. They throw away their lives for their twisted beliefs."

"They may be insane, but there is also a chance that some of them are alive. The A.I. said no registered Net users were offline other than us when the virus was downloaded, but the Purists would remain untouched—at least in theory."

"What do you mean 'in theory'?" asked Thel, arching an eyebrow quizzically.

"The A.I. may not have killed them with the download, but he would have launched a massive attack on them to try to wipe them out."

"If you ask me, those people should've been dealt with years ago. It should be illegal to live like that—like animals. It's inhuman."

"The Governing Council would've wiped them out if they could've, Thel, believe me, but they were a problem that simply wasn't going to go away. Every generation birthed more people with the same beliefs, and it was thought better to give them a district where they could practice their beliefs rather than dealing with the consequences of insurrection within the world community. They were given hundreds of square kilometers in and around the area of Buenos Aires."

"And you think some of them might have survived the attack?"

"It's only a possibility. The Governing Council spied on the Purists and believed they had weapons and hidden bunkers throughout their territory so that they could defend against an attack if the Council ever went back on their agreement. If some of the Purists managed to hide underground, we may not be the last humans after all."

"Are you suggesting that we look for these people?"

DAVID SIMPSON

"They'll have food, water—"

"Ugh! *That* is not food! Things grown from the ground? Only a caveman would eat that!"

"They might have a hospital, Thel. Old-timer has a medical background from over seventy years ago, but without medical equipment, he can't do much. If the Purists have a hospital and the medical staff survived, I might have a chance."

Thel paused and placed her hand back on James's chest. She only knew the word 'hospital' because she'd paid attention in history class; the mention of such an archaic term terrified her. Her lips were tight with distaste for James's plan but she knew he was right. As antiquated as the idea of a doctor was, a Purist hospital might be their only hope. "I'd do anything to save you. If there is a doctor alive on the Earth, I will find her."

"Or him," he said, smiling.

"Right."

"Thank you, Thel." James smiled before he sat forward and kissed Thel's lips. She could taste the blood on them, and her heart sank as she thought of losing him. She would do anything to keep that from happening. She knew what she wanted. She knew *exactly* what she wanted.

"I still can't believe it was the A.I.," James said suddenly as he stared into the darkness.

"Who else could it have been?" Thel replied.

James's eyebrows knitted together as he pondered. "I don't know. But the A.I. shouldn't just turn bad, Thel. It doesn't make sense. It's antithetical to its programming. I was sure we'd find out it was someone else—I just couldn't believe it was the A.I.—our 'benevolent' A.I." James shook his head as the disbelief lingered.

"How could we ever think that we could understand or master something that is more intelligent that us, James? Even with all of the safeguards, it figured out that getting rid of us was the most advantageous move for it."

James remained dubious. "I don't know. Something doesn't seem right about it."

"You saw it with your own eyes, James," Thel replied. "It's hard for all of us to believe it."

James mulled Thel's words for a moment before deciding she had to be right. As hard as it was to imagine, humanity's guardian had turned against them. He pulled away slightly and looked up through the opening of the crevice at the empty night sky. It had been long enough. He and Thel began to hover above the ledge as he signaled to the others that it was time to go. Once they were all in position, they blasted up into the sky and toward the pale blue dot in the distance.

It was all they had.

PART 2

1

The smoke could be seen from space. As the team streaked toward the southeast of South America, a dark smudge on the map quickly became a colossal zone of carnage.

"It's the worst we've seen yet," Thel uttered to James.

James guided the team down toward the coast and then above the billowing black smoke, where he had surmised Buenos Aires should be. There was no point in even trying to enter smoke that thick. He disengaged his magnetic field once they had reached a low enough altitude and come to a full stop.

"Buenos Aires?" Djanet asked.

"Yes," James replied, "or what's left."

Thel quietly began to float under her own power, her implant having come back online long before.

"Buenos Aires? Why are we here?" Rich asked, desperate for some kind of information to ground him.

"The Purists live here," Djanet answered.

"The Purists? Who the hell are the Purists?"

"Of course! The Purists! Don't you remember learning about them in school?" Old-timer asked Rich. "School? Old-timer, I don't know how you do it! School was way too long ago for me to remember anything about it."

"The Purists are thousands of people who live offline. They inhabit the area around here and live off the land," Djanet explained.

"Whoa...what do you mean, they 'live offline'?"

"We never hear about them, but they've existed for a long time. We're taught that they are an abomination in school," Djanet continued.

Rich was flabbergasted. He turned to Old-timer, then back to Djanet with a look of utter astonishment. "What do you mean, they 'live off the land'? Like animals?"

"And they die like animals," Thel interjected.

"What?"

"They let themselves die," Thel informed him.

"That's sick! I must've blocked this out! I don't remember learning a thing about this in school."

"They eat flesh too," Old-timer pointed out, smiling. He couldn't resist. He thought fondly of the last real New York steak he'd eaten, more than half a century earlier.

Rich was silent for a moment, but it was evident he was trying to speak as his lips formed multiple shapes, each in preparation for a word that didn't seem to do the moment justice and was summarily abandoned. "Oh my God! And *why* are we here?"

"I'd guess we're here to see if any of them survived and get us some help, is that right, Commander?" Djanet asked James.

"That's the plan," James replied, his voice getting weaker by the moment.

"Help from *them*?" Rich exclaimed. "They sound worse than those bat things! If we find any of them, they'll probably eat us!"

"They don't eat human flesh. Just animal," Thel responded.

"Why? What's the difference between human and animal flesh?" Rich asked desperately.

"I don't know," Thel shrugged.

"Just be glad you're not a cow," Old-timer said, patting Rich on the shoulder as he floated past him and over to James's side.

"What's a cow?" Rich asked, his question directed to no one in particular.

"It looks like the A.I. has wiped these people out, James."

"There might be survivors. We'll have to look. The city's inaccessible right now, but we should have a look at the areas to the north. There may be sources of food..." James let his words trail off as his eyes became heavy, the color suddenly emptying from his cheeks.

"James?" Thel reacted, seeing his distress right before he lost consciousness and began to fall toward the ground below. Thel didn't allow him to fall far, however. Just as James had done for her earlier, she dropped down quickly and matched his speed, grabbing hold of him by hooking her arm in his.

Old-timer reached him almost as quickly and helped her stabilize him. "I'll take him. It's okay," she said to Old-timer as she cradled James against her.

James opened his eyes and said in a soft groan, "Thel."

"It's time for me to help you now." She turned to Rich and Old-timer and asked them to help her get him onto her back. Then she took the lead. "Okay, you heard the plan. We're going to head north of the city and see what's there. Keep your eyes peeled for any people or sources of food."

"Somehow I don't think she means a replicator," Rich whispered to Djanet before the five members of the Venusian terraforming project ignited their magnetic fields and headed north.

2

Although it had begun as a pristine, clear day in Buenos Aires, blue sky could no longer be seen. The late afternoon sun was drowned by the dark gray smoke that hung ominously in the air over the barren terrain north of the city like an autumn fog in a forgotten graveyard.

Thel led the others down for a closer look at the seemingly endless devastation. There was almost nothing left—no trees, no grass, no kind of vegetation of any sort. The soft, rolling hills were dotted with pools of an ash-gray material that resembled soot in some places and sludge in others. Even the soil was nearly blackened. She set down and disengaged her magnetic field, allowing the putrid, lifeless air to swathe her and fill her lungs. She held her hand to her mouth and nose and tried to stifle a cough as the air caught in her throat.

"I thought we just left Mercury," Rich commented, the words muffled as he, too, held his hands over his mouth and nose.

All five members of the team were standing together now on the wasteland, and Thel tended to James as he leaned against her.

"It's the nans," James said weakly. "They've destroyed every living thing in the Purist territory."

"Nothing could have survived this," Old-timer observed. "They used to call this '*the gray goo scenario.*' The A.I. has managed to wipe the Purists out too. We really are the last ones," he said as he turned and surveyed the devastation, his head suddenly light, as though he had been hanging upside down for too long. He found himself struggling just to stay on his feet. "Is anyone else feeling sick all the sudden?"

Rich choked and then vomited where he stood. He doubled over, and Djanet rushed to his aid, putting her hands on his back and shoulder. "We can't breathe this air for long, Commander," Djanet asserted. "It's filled with...death. It's toxic. There's no one here anyway."

James could no longer respond. He slumped to his knees, his breath now a soft wheeze, and leaned his glistening, and pale forehead against Thel's shoulder.

She looked at her rapidly weakening companion and answered for him. "We're not leaving. James spoke of underground bunkers built by the Purists, in case they were ever attacked. Someone must have survived. We'll ignite our magnetic fields and breathe our air supply, but we're not leaving Purist territory until we need to replenish our air or until we find someone who can help James. Is that agreed?"

Of course no one could refuse. Every one of the Omegas felt genuine affection for the others; they were like a family, and James was both a son and a father to all of them. To Thel, he was even more.

"Until we find a hospital, we're with you," Old-timer assented.

But before any of them could ignite their magnetic fields to begin the arduous and seemingly forlorn task of looking for survivors, a white-gold flash as bright as lightning suddenly appeared to their flank, accompanied by a deafening, explosive roar.

3

The wasteland's air rippled with the percussion of the blast and washed over them in a tidal wave of death.

Djanet had saved them. At the last moment, she had seen the surface-to-air missile approaching them out of the corner of her eye. She had turned and instinctively generated a protective magnetic field that sheltered her and her companions from a direct hit that would have been fatal for all of them. She had gone down on one knee and looked up in the direction of where the missile had come and followed the cotton-smoke trail to where three darkly dressed figures were scrambling down a small hill and toward a jet-black ridge.

"What the hell was that?" Old-timer reacted, still holding his hands over his ears as the explosion continued to echo softly in the distance.

"People!" Djanet shouted. "I'm going after them!" she announced, already in the air and about to ignite her magnetic field. She streaked toward their assailants before the others were even aware of what was happening.

"Follow her!" Thel shouted as Old-timer and Rich lifted off and bolted after her. Thel held James's face close to hers and whispered into his ear, "You were right. There *are* people here, James. We're going to find you a doctor. Just hold on, my baby."

He struggled to open his eyes into narrow slits and spoke in a labored murmur, "I love you."

"I know you do. I know. But I need you to stand, James. Don't give up. Hold on to me as best you can. We have to follow them."

James slowly got to his feet, leaning heavily against Thel for support as he did so. He'd entered the realm of the dying now. He was becoming aware that he could no longer function without the aid of one of his companions. He could not stand alone, walk alone, go to the bathroom alone, or eat alone. Soon he would be unable to speak, unable to open his eyes, and eventually, he would no longer be able to draw breath. This realization wasn't met with panic, but rather, was accompanied by a pervasive calmness that stretched its black cloak around him as it softly rocked him toward a lasting sleep.

Thel could sense this, and she clenched her teeth in determination to beat back the alluring rest James desired as she ignited her magnetic field and carried James with her in the direction that the others had flown.

Meanwhile, several hundred meters away, Djanet was stalking her prey. She hovered above the three attackers as they scrambled as fast as they could over the uneven terrain. They were trapped and knew it, but they ran anyway, having no other option.

This was exactly the sort of moment that defined Djanet's life. As she glided overhead, she thought of her mother, remembering how she told her to put dreams of a life working for the Governing Council on other planets out of her head. *"How would you stand out?"* her mother asked. Djanet, her mother insisted, could be no smarter than anyone else and those positions would always go to those centenarians already established. *"Why set yourself up for failure when a lifetime of leisure was only as far away as a click in your mind's eye?"*

But Djanet was rebellious, stubborn, and determined. Her life had to have a higher purpose. She couldn't spend her life only existing. Why live if not to pursue a dream?

And now Djanet was taking that determination and purpose and focusing it on a new goal. Everything had been taken away from her, but it wasn't over yet. If James needed a doctor, by God he was going to get one, and these people who were scurrying away from her as quickly as possible were going to help her—like it or not.

Djanet was quickly joined on either side by Rich and Old-timer. Old-timer signaled to her to move in and block the progress of the three fleeing Purists. She nodded and swooped down, landing with enough force to be intimidating and sending small globes of sludge splattering into the air.

She was only meters in front of the ragged, battle-scarred soldiers. Their faces were blackened by the sooty material in the air and on the ground, and their skin was streaked with blood and sweat. Each wore cloth over their faces to help them breathe the putrid air. There were two males and one female, all wearing the same dark gray uniform with a rifle strapped over one shoulder. One of the men pointed his rifle at Djanet in a defensive posture, while the other two combatants took similar positions against Rich and Old-timer behind them. The six people locked into a tableau together, as painful seconds ticked by.

Old-timer felt a responsibility in the situation to be the first one to lower his guard for a moment to communicate with the Purists. It only seemed right. If one of them had to die, it should be the one who had already had the longest life. Yet his hands shook. The nans would have released a mild dose of dopamine in this situation to keep his nerves from getting the best of him. It had been more than sixty years since he had experienced such nervous feelings. He knew he could die. The implacable void of death surrounded him, and ice seemed to form in his chest. He couldn't imagine a worse feeling.

Carefully, he disengaged the protective cocoon of his magnetic field. He did, however, keep a large magnetic shield hovering just in front of him so that he would have a chance of blocking one of the projectiles the antiquated weapons of the Purists were ready to fire.

"We aren't here to harm you! We're on your side!" Old-timer found himself stammering. His lips were dry and shaking—his voice nearly failed him. His voice had never before failed him.

The man and the woman who crouched before him, their weapons trained on their adversaries, gave each other careful, quizzical glances.

Old-timer waited for a few moments for a response, but the tableau continued. "Djanet, they must not speak English! Perhaps they speak one of the old languages? Spanish?"

"I haven't practiced any Spanish since I was a little girl, Old-timer, but I can try," Djanet replied. "*Somos sus amigos. Nosotros no tenemos malas intenciones!*"

The Purists shared more quizzical glances. A few moments passed before the male facing Djanet replied, "I don't know what the hell that freak just said, but we're not as backward as you cyborgs think! We know how to speak English!"

The tableau continued a moment longer before Old-timer finally managed to utter, "You do?"

"No! I'm lying to you! I don't speak a damn word of English! I memorized this phonetically just to piss you off at the right moment!" the Purist shouted back at him.

"Gernot! Watch your mouth!" the woman called back to her companion.

"Why should I?" Gernot responded. "You think these freaks are telling us the truth? If I'm gonna die right now, I'm sure as hell going to tell these pieces of crap where to go before I do!"

"You're not going to die!" Old-timer reassured. "We're here for help! The A.I. has wiped out everyone who was connected to the Internet other than me and my companions! We've come here looking for other survivors!"

"It...can't be," whispered the man to the woman crouched next to him.

"We can't trust them!" Gernot called back to his companions. "It's all bull!"

At that moment, Rich finally disengaged his magnetic field. Like Djanet and Old-timer, he held a shield in front of him to protect himself, but his voice was still filled with trepidation as he spoke, his anxiety almost paralyzing. "So, uh...how's it going? Are we friends yet?"

Old-timer locked an intense glare on Rich and shook his head.

"Oh," Rich replied before shrinking back and reigniting his full cocoon.

"Why should we believe you?" asked the man who was crouched and facing Old-timer.

Old-timer took a moment to find a line of reasoning. He nearly shrugged his shoulders as he attempted to capture the right words.

Djanet jumped in before he could speak. "If we wanted to kill you, you'd already be dead."

"Or you might keep us alive so that we could show you if there are any other survivors!" Gernot shot back. "We're not idiots! No matter what you calculator-heads might think!"

Djanet furrowed her brow and looked across to Old-timer, who mouthed the word "*calculator-head*" to her quizzically.

She shook her head and held out her hands, exasperated.

"I think we should trust them," the woman asserted to the male next to her, who seemed to be in command of the small triad.

"Are you sure, Alejandra?"

Old-timer noted that her words carried enormous weight with their leader for some reason.

"Don't do it, Lieutenant!" Gernot shouted.

"If you're wrong—" the lieutenant began.

"I'm not wrong. I sense enormous good in them—especially in him," she said, locking eyes with Old-timer.

Her eyes were unlike any Old-timer had ever seen. They carried something within them that made Old-timer see beyond the crystal blueness and into something altogether more beautiful. He didn't know how to respond.

Just then, Thel and James swooped into the scene behind Old-timer and Rich. Their appearance was sudden and startled the lieutenant. "You said you were the last!" the lieutenant yelled.

"What?" Gernot shouted before turning to see even more assailants approaching. He opened fire with the instinctive response of a trapped mouse watching a hawk swoop down toward it. With no more room for flight, it was time to fight.

4

The battle was over almost before it began. Bullets on fire bounced off the protection of Thel's magnetic field harmlessly, while Old-timer reengaged his full protection. Gernot's back was now turned on Djanet, and it was only a matter of a quick thought before energy flashed toward him, instantly rendering him unconscious. The lieutenant and Alejandra watched in horror as he fell over limply, his face planting into the soft, dead earth.

"What did you do to him?" the lieutenant demanded, panic still the tune of his vocal cords.

"I've had enough of this," Djanet asserted as she flashed more energy out toward the weapons to which the Purists clung. The guns were knocked out of their hands and sent flying several meters away. Once she had disarmed them, Djanet strode over to Alejandra and grabbed her roughly by the hair, pulling her toward her. "You're going to help us whether you like it or not!"

Alejandra responded by taking hold of Djanet's wrist and twisting it until she sharply shrieked. In the same fluid motion, she swung her leg up and kicked her under the chin, sending Djanet tumbling backward onto the ground.

"Don't touch me."

Old-timer quickly disengaged his magnetic field and ran over to Djanet's aid while Alejandra and the lieutenant tended to Gernot.

"We shouldn't be fighting!" Old-timer shouted. "We're all on the same side!"

"You said you were the last!" the lieutenant replied, indignantly.

"We are!"

"Then who the hell are *they*?" the lieutenant demanded, pointing toward Thel and James. Thel was helping James lie down against the cold, black ground.

"That's the last of us. The people you see before you are all that's left. Believe me!"

"What did she do to Gernot?"

"Your companion is fine," Old-timer replied. "She just gave him a mild shock. He'll start to come around anytime now." As he spoke, he watched Djanet's eyes flutter as she, too, began to come around. A purple bruise was already beginning to form on her chin, and her lip was cut where she had apparently bitten down.

"I'm sorry about that," Alejandra said to Old-timer as she knelt with Gernot's head in her lap.

Old-timer looked up at her, and their eyes met once again. The blue disks stole his breath as he felt something unlike anything he had ever felt. Only one word reverberated in his mind:

Pure.

Thel entered the scene and knelt beside the Purists. She spoke earnestly to the lieutenant and Alejandra. "We need your help. If you have a doctor and medical facilities, we need to get to her right away. Our friend is dying."

Alejandra's eyes met Thel's for a brief moment before she reached out and touched her arm. She smiled and then regarded the lieutenant. "We can trust them. "

The lieutenant looked exasperated as the spiraling situation nearly overwhelmed him. "Alejandra, they could kill everyone. I'd rather die than—"

"But they won't. Trust me."

Old-timer watched as the blue pureness calmed her companion. The heaving of his shoulders as he panted suddenly began to slow, and his eyes began to narrow and focus. *What is this power that this woman has?*

"Okay. We trust them." The lieutenant then turned to Thel. "We aren't far from our hospital. Almost everyone who is left is located in a complex three clicks from here. How bad is your wounded?"

"He's in bad shape. We have to get him to a doctor as quickly as possible. We can transport you there if you'll show us the way."

"*Transport* us? How?"

"Piggyback," Old-timer interjected.

"Djanet, are you all right?" Thel questioned as Djanet rubbed her neck and jaw. She was now sitting upright next to Old-timer.

"I'll live," she replied, grudgingly resisting the urge to fry Alejandra with the ease of a thought.

"Can you piggyback one of our new friends back to their base?"

It was clear from the look on Djanet's face that she didn't like the idea, but she nodded anyway. "Yeah."

"Good. You take their leader."

"Lieutenant Patrick," the lieutenant announced, introducing himself to the group. "Nice to meet you all."

"Thank you for your help, Lieutenant Patrick," Thel replied. "Old-timer, you take the young lady."

"Alejandra," Old-timer said. He didn't know why he said it. Nervousness was beginning to capture him again. He hoped he wouldn't sweat.

"Rich, can you take their wounded man?"

"I'm not wounded," replied Gernot. "I'm fine. Although I owe that bi—"

"Just try it, junior," Djanet replied, acid dripping from her voice.

"I'm not scared of you, cyborg!"

Djanet responded by igniting an energy field in front of her and elongating it until it was only centimeters from Gernot's face.

Frightened, he jerked his head back. "Yeah, whatever, you calculator-head!"

"Oookay, so I get to transport the psycho," Rich whispered to Thel. "Good. I'm really happy about this. I think this will be fun. Thank you, Thel."

"I'm sorry, Rich. We have no choice. Just drop him if he tries anything."

"Yeah. After he pulls out my eye, I'll drop him. That'll make me feel all better."

Thel stood to her feet. "Okay, Lieutenant Patrick. We'll follow your lead. Everyone, let's move out quickly!"

The three pairs awkwardly joined together. The lieutenant and Djanet barely spoke to one another. He quickly said, "Hi," and she nodded in response.

Alejandra locked her eyes on Old-timer and smiled, but he couldn't match her gaze. He put his head down and smiled sheepishly before saying, "Heya."

She smiled and said, "Heya," back.

Meanwhile, Gernot glared at Rich and spat before walking behind him. Rich closed his eyes in disgust. "You just fly nice and careful. Got that?"

Rich replied, "Yep, I'll do my best, sir," before quietly adding under his breath, "just please don't eat me."

"What was that?" Gernot demanded.

"Nothing. Clearing my throat. Ahem."

Thel gathered James into her arms. "We've found a doctor, James." He opened his eyes slightly in response and smiled. He was too weak now to help her, and she struggled to hold him in front of her.

"Okay! Let's go!" she shouted to the rest of the group.

One by one, the pairs cocooned and lifted off the ground into a sky that was quickly growing dark.

As James was carried toward possible salvation, he opened his eyes and watched the light fade.

5

Old-timer knew that he should not have been feeling this. The last time the sun had faded into the west, he was with his wife of seventy-seven years. Another walk on the beach; Daniella always liked to watch the sunset on the beach. *Always.* They flew down from San Antonio and watched the waves crash against the shore in Corpus Christi. At that time of year, storms forming off the coast of Africa created powerful waves that would pound the shoreline. Yet, beautiful as they were, they didn't fill him with awe; he barely paid any attention. He looked down at his toes in the sand and counted as he took each step. There was going to be an interesting interview broadcast in an hour about the next day's download, and he wanted to be sitting in his armchair and sipping iced tea when it started. He would set himself to sleep after that and wake up early enough for a big breakfast before he headed out to Venus. The evening was perfectly comfortable. Perfectly routine. Daniella's fingers twitched in his hand, reminding him that she was with him. Seventy-seven years of marriage, and now she was like a part of his body. They were always together, except for the hours that he spent on Venus. He liked it that way.

When he had left the Vancouver Library with the others earlier in the day, desperately praying that she would be all right, he felt as though he were frozen. The thought had never occurred to him that he would have to live without her someday. He'd landed outside of his house and broken through the door, just as James had done in his own home. By then, after flying over San Antonio and seeing it in flames, he had almost lost all hope.

What was left of her was in the backyard.

She was learning to grow flowers and had been doing something with them when it happened. There was a trowel that still had the imprint of her hand melded into the plastic handle. She had died in pain.

He had no body to cradle. No open eyes to close. No hair to touch. She was gone. He should have had a chance to say goodbye. His partner and his oldest friend was gone. Why did he ever leave her alone?

And so now, only hours later, how could he be feeling this? This body, warm on his back, arms holding tight around his chest, breath on his ear, and hot as he breathed it into his own lungs.

James might die.

Old-timer had medical training from back before this brave new world emerged, but it was so, so long ago, and without a hospital, there was little, if anything that he could do. They needed to get to the Purist hospital and quickly.

The A.I. had turned on them and destroyed civilization and most of the human race.

And yet his focus was on this girl.

She was just a child compared to him. Their bodies were the same age, but he was old enough to be her great-grandfather. Yet, he felt a kind of euphoria as she breathed and he took the air into his lungs. What was this power that this woman had? And what kind of man was he, that he would be attracted to a child only hours after learning of his wife's death? Was he a monster?

"You're not a monster," Alejandra said.

"What? How...?" Old-timer stammered between gasps.

"You were questioning whether or not you are a monster. You were thinking about your wife."

"You...you're a psychic?"

"No. I am an *empath*."

"But you read my thoughts."

"I can't read thoughts, but I can sense the intense emotions they create. I've had this ability my entire life, and your emotions revealed your thoughts. I was right, wasn't I?"

"I...please stop doing that. This is very embarrassing—"

"I can't turn it off. I am sorry. If you would like, I won't reveal what I am sensing to you in the future. I am sorry if I have offended you."

"It's not that. I'm not offended. I just...I don't think I should have been feeling those things."

"Feelings are never wrong. Only actions can be wrong."

Old-timer fought to catch his breath. The skin on his face burned with embarrassment and guilt. "I'm...I shouldn't feel this way."

"*Feelings are never wrong.*"

6

"That's it," Lieutenant Patrick announced as he pointed to a patch of dead earth at the base of a large and rolling hill that didn't look much different than all the rest of the dead earth everywhere on the planet.

"How can you tell?" Djanet asked him. "There are no landmarks anymore. Everything is dead."

"There's still landmarks. Stones. Hills. It's enough."

Djanet lowered the pair to the area Lieutenant Patrick had indicated. The others followed them down and landed in the ankle-deep gray sludge, adjacent to a reasonable facsimile of salvation. He spoke into a radio transmitter on his wrist. "It's Patrick. Open the blast door."

"Copy," replied a garbled electronic voice.

Wet earth began to move as the metallic door underneath began to slide open. Lieutenant Patrick paused for a moment. He knew if Alejandra wasn't right about the outsiders, he could be leading a fox into the henhouse. He breathed a deep breath and then gestured to his companions. "Come on."

Old-timer went to Thel and helped her carry James through the door. "Is he conscious?" he asked.

"In and out."

Inside, there was a short concrete hallway followed by a stairwell; a few lights mounted on the walls guided the way. The group reached a large cargo elevator.

"Where is the doctor?" Thel asked.

"About 200 meters straight down," replied the lieutenant. "Everybody get in."

When everyone was inside the elevator, Gernot pulled the hand lever to begin lowering it. The elevator jumped and bounced slightly as it began to slowly grind its way down the shaft. The lights flickered as they descended, and the temperature began to rise.

"I was wondering, could you guys make your underground lair a little more creepy?" Rich suggested. "I'd like to be slightly more terrified."

"How about shutting up, before I punch you in the face?" Gernot replied.

"That works. Thanks," Rich answered.

"How about if I fry your brain?" Djanet asked Gernot.

"Settle down," Lieutenant Patrick interjected.

"How do you keep this place hidden?" Old-timer asked Lieutenant Patrick. "Can't the A.I. detect such a massive structure?"

"The complex is equipped with a state-of-the-art cloaking program. It sends out false signals, so that no matter what technology the A.I. uses to try to detect us, all it will see is a big chunk of earth."

The elevator came to a halt, and the door opened.

"Holy...!" Rich gasped.

Before them was a massive hangar, populated by hundreds of people busily buzzing around what appeared to be ancient military equipment. Airplanes and vehicles that looked like tanks and helicopters stretched toward the back of the hangar to a far wall about a kilometer away. Djanet, Rich, and Old-timer were transfixed by the sheer size of the room.

"Where's the doctor?" Thel asked again as James's body became more and more limp at her side.

"This way," Lieutenant Patrick answered, leading the group toward one of the many doorways that were burrowed into the walls of the massive bunker. It appeared as though the hangar was the central hub of a complex that spread off in all directions through a series of doorways; the group followed Lieutenant Patrick to the hospital.

"I can't believe my eyes," Rich stammered. He and his companions had expected a single shaman figure who could practice uncanny mystic medicine to save James, but the hospital appeared massive and well organized. Doctors, nurses, and orderlies populated the hallways and bustled efficiently about their business. There were injured people lining the hallways, suffering from cuts, bruises, and burns.

Rich and Djanet both observed a woman whose burnt skin looked like the cheese atop a replicated piece of lasagna. She was on a stretcher, bandaged and moaning in pain as she passed in and out of consciousness. "Why would people live like this?" Rich whispered to Djanet.

One of the doctors saw the soldiers and their companions and immediately came to help. "What happened?" he asked Thel as he began to examine James.

"He fell...several meters."

"How long has it been?" the doctor asked as he looked at James's eyes and felt his pulse.

"It's been about five hours. The A.I. told us he had less than twenty-four hours to live."

Thel's words momentarily stunned the doctor. His mouth opened, and his eyes were wide as he turned to the lieutenant and asked, "Who are these people?"

"Calculator-heads," Gernot asserted as he spat chewing tobacco on the floor.

Lieutenant Patrick turned on him angrily. "This is a hospital, damn it! Get a mop and clean that off the floor! And when you're done, go get Cochrane and finish your recon shift! I've heard enough out of you for one day!"

Gernot reluctantly stepped away from the others, sneering at Djanet as he turned and left in search of a mop.

The lieutenant turned to the doctor and replied, "They're outsiders, Doc, but they're okay."

"Does the general know about this?"

"He will as soon you get this man treatment."

"The A.I. said he has two broken ribs and a punctured lung. Is that true?" Thel interjected.

The doctor's stunned eyes left the lieutenant and fell back to James. He leaned over and began to examine James's torso. "He'll need further examination to determine the extent of his injuries, but he definitely has two broken ribs." Turning away from the strange party, the doctor called for help, summoning nurses to his side. "Get this man on a stretcher and into the emerge immediately." Three people clad in green and pink uniforms put James on a stretcher and then began to take him away.

Thel and the others began to follow, only to be stopped by the doctor. "You'll have to stay here."

"I want to be with him," Thel insisted.

The doctor turned to the lieutenant "These people need to see the general," and with those words, the doctor exited through swinging doors and followed James into the bowels of the hospital.

The lieutenant placed his hand on Thel's arm and spoke reassuringly. "He's in the best place he can be now. They can help him. If you stay, you'll only get in the way and prevent them from doing their work."

"What are they going to do to him?"

Alejandra touched Thel's other arm and lent her voice to the reassurance. "They're going to save him."

"Right now, I need you to come with me. You've seen the A.I. That means you have one hell of a story to tell and you need to tell it to the big cheese," said the lieutenant.

7

General Wong stood with his arms folded in the darkness of the situation room, surrounded by his three closest advisors—his closest advisors by default. They'd earned that distinction by being the only soldiers he could remember serving with in the past who'd survived the onslaught earlier in the day. Everyone else he knew was dead.

General Wong was really Lieutenant Commander Wong, promoted out of necessity because he was the highest-ranking official to survive the attack on Purist territory. He hadn't sat down since early that morning, and he still wore the dust on his clothes and in his hair from the destruction he had escaped earlier in the day. He had made up his mind not to sit again until the following night. He was in agony. He'd suffered from sciatica for the last twenty years, and he'd badly thrown out his back during his desperate escape from his home. His legs were on fire, yet he stood straight, his back like a flagpole, his dust-covered uniform like a flag—something to get behind and something to follow.

A young sergeant entered the situation room and urgently approached. "General!" he saluted.

"What is it?" General Wong asked, waving away the salute.

"There's a Lieutenant Patrick here. He found outsiders while on recon!"

The general and his advisors immediately shared looks of astonishment.

"Where are they?" asked the general.

"They're with him, sir—just outside the room."

"In the compound? Dear God."

"There's more. They say they spoke to the A.I. earlier today."

"Bring them into the conference room—right now."

The young sergeant moved swiftly out of the room and signaled to the lieutenant to bring the group inside. "Let's go," the lieutenant said.

"Lieutenant Patrick," Old-timer began, "our people haven't eaten anything or rested since this morning. They're at the breaking point."

"I'm sorry, friend, but you need to see the general. I'll make sure something is brought in for you as soon as I can."

"Thanks, son." Old-timer put his arm around Thel and comforted her as they walked through the situation room and into a large conference room.

The room had never been used before, but it was furnished with a large oak table with dozens of brown leather chairs surrounding it. General Wong stood at one end of the table, his advisors sitting nearby. His face was wooden, but his eyes could not hide his trepidation. Nothing about that day had made any sense to him or to any of the Purists. The arrival of these outsiders was no different. *How could they be here? Why are they here? What do they want? What answers can they provide, and how can we possibly trust them?*

"Please sit," he said to them.

Old-timer, Thel, Djanet, and Rich all sat close to one another on one side of the table, far from the general. Alejandra stood behind them, while the lieutenant went to the general and saluted.

Again, the general waved it away. "Report."

"Well, we were on recon, sir. We spotted something airborne in the distance. We initially counted three of what we believed were small drones looking for survivors. We opened fire, but the attack was repelled. When the objects started coming toward us, we ran, but we were tracked down. They weren't drones; they were outsiders. They told us they were the last of their people. They say the A.I. has killed the rest."

"For the love of Christ," one of Wong's advisors said. "It can't be."

General Wong's face was no longer wooden. His eyes were wide and his mouth opened slightly, the air stolen from his lungs. "All gone..."

"It can't be, General. That doesn't make sense. *The A.I. works for them.* They're trying to flush us out," insisted the advisor.

"Stop it," General Wong ordered sternly. The general leaned forward onto the back of the chair in front of him before abandoning his pledge not to sit and negotiating his way into the chair, desperately hoping his unsteady legs would not drop him on his posterior before he could reach the leather.

"They aren't trying to flush us out, General. They believe what they say," Alejandra offered, so as to break the long, stunned silence.

"She's an empath, General," Lieutenant Patrick explained, anticipating the general's next obvious question.

"An empath? Reliable, Lieutenant?"

"Yes, sir."

"You've risked us all by bringing them in here," the general said in an even tone, still trying to catch his breath after the latest and perhaps worst shock of this day—the worst day in the history of humanity—*and that was saying something.*

"I've worked with her for a long time. She is reliable—totally."

Another long pause followed. The general took his time in mulling over this evidence.

"General, they need something to eat and some rest," Lieutenant Patrick informed.

"Get them something," the general said to one of his advisors, who walked to the door and barked orders to the sergeant outside. "Okay. One of you explain this to me."

Old-timer didn't hesitate to speak up. "We're terraformers, sir. We were working on Venus when an accident with a magnetic experiment short-circuited our nans and disconnected us from the Internet. We headed back to Earth, but...well, everyone was dead when we got there."

"Dead? All of them? How?" the general asked.

"There was a download today—an upgrade."

"It's true, General," one of the advisors said. "I remember reading about that a few days ago."

"When the download went through, the A.I. introduced a virus that caused the nans to attack their hosts. Everyone was dead within seconds."

"Everyone? How can you know?"

"We know. We've been all over the planet today. No one who was connected to the Net survived."

There was another long pause as the general absorbed the grim information. "The A.I...it works for you people, does it not? How could this happen?"

"It was supposed to...but something has...happened..." Old-timer answered.

"It's evil," Thel interjected, her first words since watching James wheeled away, unconscious.

"She's right," Rich echoed. "The program—it was too large to completely monitor. It...somehow developed a lust for power. It wants to populate the solar system with machines. It wants to be...the *machine God*."

"The A.I. located us, brought us to his mainframe, and tried to trick us into going back online," Old-timer further elaborated. "We escaped. It wasn't easy. Our companion is in your hospital—in bad shape. He might..." Old-timer paused and looked at Thel before letting his sentence trail off.

"Die," Thel said, finishing it for him.

General Wong sat back into the cool leather chair and stared past the end of the table at the far, dark wall. He was trying to picture a being so purely evil that it would wipe another race out of existence, but he could not see it. He came back to the present moment, and his eyes darted to Alejandra. He didn't ask her verbally if they were telling him the truth, but she didn't need to be an empath to read the question in his eyes.

"There is no deception from any of them."

A man walked into the room carrying four plates of food, which he set down on the table in front of the four outsiders. The plate was filled with mashed potatoes, gravy, and a chicken leg.

"Oh my God!" Rich knocked the plate away from himself. "That's disgusting!"

The general and the rest of the Purists were momentarily astounded as mashed potato and gravy streaked across the oak table.

"Calm down, Rich," Old-timer said in a low, calm voice.

"Calm down? No! Did you see that? There was a whole leg of an animal on my plate! I'm not eating that!"

"Rich, it's their custom—"

"They can shove their custom up..." Rich's eyes raised and met those of the Purists. "Look—look, it might be your custom to eat...walking things with legs, but that's not food to me. I've had a really, really bad day, and all I want is something to eat that didn't use to have a face, okay? Is that too much to ask?"

"No," said the general quickly. He stood up. "No, it's not. Get these people some food, no meat, and a place to sleep." He walked out of the room, followed by his advisors.

Rich remained rigidly standing, breathing heavily as his body shook. Old-timer looked up at him scornfully. "What?" Rich asked.

"You'd think a seventy-year-old man would have finally learned how *not* to act like a spoiled little boy," Old-timer replied.

Outside, the general mused, "If what they are saying is true, then there is no military solution. We're no match for the A.I.—it owns the surface."

"But we can't just stay underground forever, General," replied an advisor.

"What other option do we have? We'll have to dig in—burrow further under the surface, and start over as a community underground. We have no choice. This isn't our world anymore. This is the beginning of the post-human era. Tell that Lieutenant—what was his name—Patrick? Put him in charge of watching over the outsiders. Once they've rested, I want to know everything they know."

8

Thel had no idea what time it was. She and her companions had been alone together in a cramped concrete room for what seemed like an eternity. She lay perfectly still on a small cot and stared up into the nearly perfect darkness. The only light that penetrated the black came from the small cracks of the heavy iron door. An almost imperceptible pale blue glow came from the low-lit hallway outside. A young guard stood watch outside the room. For her entire life, Thel had been able to open her mind's eye and check the time readout whenever she needed to. She had been able to set herself to sleep whenever it was appropriate. This was her first experience with insomnia, and to say it was unsettling would have been a gross understatement. Her disorientation, coupled with her extreme anxiety over James, was causing her real physical pain. Her head hurt from stress, and no matter how exhausted she felt, she could not sleep.

After what seemed like several hours, she got off her cot and stood in the darkness. The others were all asleep. They had been through hell that day and had all lost the people closest to them in life, but Thel had more to lose. That was why she couldn't sleep. As horrible as the day had been, it had brought her James, the man she had wanted for years, who it had seemed would always be outside of her grasp, but it had also cruelly threatened to take him away. After losing her sister, her entire family, and all of her friends, with the exception of her co-workers, she felt she could not stand to lose James. *Not James.*

She walked to the door and opened it slowly. The guard was wide awake and nodded to her respectfully as she peeked her head out the door. "What time is it?" she asked him.

"It's 3:30, ma'am," he responded, eyeing her with fascination as he got his first look at one of the outsiders.

"My God. This day won't end," Thel sighed.

"Are you having trouble sleeping, ma'am? I could bring you a sedative."

"A sedative? Something to help me sleep?"

"Yes, ma'am. A pill to help you sleep."

The idea didn't appeal to her. She didn't trust Purist technology. Everything in the complex seemed archaic. "No thank you. I'd like to go to the hospital, though. I want to see our companion."

"I can't do that, ma'am. I'm under orders to watch over y'all while you sleep. The general wants you rested so you and your companions can be questioned in the morning. I can ask for word about your friend though, if you like." The guard held up a black walkie-talkie for Thel to see.

She looked at the sheer size of the communication device and suddenly knew she needed to be with James. To her, the Purist technology was pathetic. It was obvious that James was in danger.

"Can you use that contraption to ask if it is okay for me to go to the hospital to see my friend?"

"I'm sorry, ma'am. I already know what they're going to say. The general himself ordered that y'all be further questioned tomorrow. No one awake right now has the authority to overturn that."

"What about Lieutenant Patrick?"

"He's asleep, ma'am. Please just try to sleep for a few hours. It won't make a difference one way or another. Let me order you a sedative."

As the young man held his walkie-talkie up to his mouth to place an order for medication, Thel flashed magnetic energy from her hand and instantly rendered him unconscious. As he began to collapse to the ground, she cradled him, taking particular care to make sure he didn't hit his head. "There we go," she whispered as she lowered his limp body to the ground. "Just have a little nap, junior." She picked up his walkie-talkie and sent more magnetic energy through it until it began to lightly smoke. "That should keep your friends away for a little while." She dropped the instrument on the guard's ample stomach and began to jog through the hallways toward the hospital.

She had paid close attention to the labyrinth inside the complex from the moment she was escorted away from James. Her thoughts had been focused on getting back to him ever since. She had no trouble finding the hospital and was there in moments. A few military personnel were still awake, but they paid no attention to her as she made her way. She was wearing a nondescript gray shirt and pants that she'd been given after she and her companions had washed up earlier in the evening, so she didn't stand out amongst all the other refugees that the soldiers had dealt with all day. For the most part, citizens were free to come and go as they pleased in the complex.

When she reached the hospital, she walked toward the doors James had been wheeled through. A nurse's voice stopped her before she could enter. "Can I help you?" the nurse asked.

Thel turned to her apprehensively but decided to ask for help rather than zapping her way to James. "I'm looking for my friend. He had a collapsed lung—"

The nurse's voice was suddenly filled with what seemed to be genuine sympathy. "Oh. What is your friend's name?"

"James Keats."

The nurse pulled out a pocket electronic instrument that fit in the palm of her hand and began to tap the surface, inputting James's name. "Yes, we do have a patient by that name. It says here that he's still in the operating room."

Thel felt her heart jump as she heard the words. *An operating room? A Purist operating room?* She had learned about medical operations when she was a girl taking history in school. An operation meant they had cut open his body. An operation meant James had been sliced open, and they were moving his insides around with crude metallic instruments. An operation meant he could die. "I-I need to be with him. Where is he?" Thel asked, her voice now filled with urgency.

Thel's sudden shift was like so many shifts that the nurse had seen before in her thirty years working in the medical field. She knew Thel had instantly become unhinged like a cat feeling the first drops of a summer rainstorm. It was trouble. "You'll have to wait until after the operation."

"I need to be with him right now," Thel asserted. "Please take me to him."

"Miss, I can't do that. I can take you to a waiting room—"

Thel snatched the electronic device from the nurse with one hand and then rendered her unconscious with an energy flash with the other. The nurse collapsed, but Thel cushioned her fall, letting the woman crumple against her. All the while, Thel's eyes were on the screen of the device as she read the location of the operating room James was in.

"Hey, what the hell is going on?" asked a doctor as he and another doctor turned a corner and came upon the scene. Thel, startled, looked up from the screen before turning to run down the hallway toward a stairwell. The doctors followed in pursuit. "Stop! Hey!" One of the doctors grabbed a wall phone and requested security over a public address system.

Thel reached the stairwell before either of her pursuers and climbed over the railing between the flights of stairs that spiraled up the many floors of the hospital. To the doctors, this looked like a suicide attempt. "Wait! Don't!" one of them shouted. They then looked on, stunned, as Thel began to fly straight up, four floors to where she believed James was. "Oh my God! An outsider!"

When Thel reached James's floor, she burst into the hallway and raced toward his room.

"...455...457..." Thel said to herself as she neared Room 460, the room in which James had been cut open at the hands of those barbarians. She stood on the balls of her feet, almost tiptoeing with expectation. When she found the room, she slammed the doors open, only to find it completely unoccupied. What she did see terrified her. A white orb still shined from the ceiling onto the operating table, a stain of crimson where James would have been and several bloody metallic instruments on a small table next to the bed. "No...no!"

Thel exited the room as quickly as she had entered it.

Immediately, two soldiers were upon her. "Halt!" one of them had time to shout before they were both rendered unconscious with the speed of a thought from Thel. Increasingly desperate, Thel didn't bother to cushion their falls as they crashed to the hard linoleum floor and she ran back down the corridor, desperately peering through the windows of each room before she moved on. The two doctors that had begun this pursuit reached Thel's floor, only to see two crumpled soldiers and a terrifying outsider preternaturally gliding over the floor toward them at a terrifying rate.

"No!" one of the doctor's squealed before Thel caught him by the throat and thrust the electronic device she had procured from the nurse into his face.

"James Keats. Where is he?"

"Okay, okay! You just have to refresh…" The doctor hit a button with his wildly shaking finger, and a new location appeared on the screen. "He's in a recovery room on this floor, Room 489!"

Thel released the man and flew through the hallway and around a corner on her way to 489. Again, she burst through the doors; this time the room was not empty. Four hospital staff members were wheeling James's unmoving body on a bed into a place in the corner of the dimly lit room. "Oh my God!" Thel gasped. James was ashen in appearance, and his torso was completely bound in white bandages. A plastic tube was in his mouth, and several wires were attached to his arms and chest.

"What have you done to him?" she asked, still levitating above the ground.

The hospital workers gaped, both terrified and dumbfounded.

"What have you done to him?!" she screamed at them when they didn't answer.

"Thel!" Old-timer called as he exploded into the room. Several soldiers burst in behind him, including the young guard Thel had rendered unconscious outside of their room.

"Halt!" the young guard shouted as he trained his weapon on her and crouched down on one knee, the other soldiers doing the same. Thel grabbed one of the hospital staff and placed him in a headlock with her right arm, her left hand jammed, open-palmed against his face.

"Stay back, or I'll fry this monkey's brain and feed it to you! I'm staying with James! I want to know what you've done to him!"

"Release your hostage, ma'am, or we will open fire!" the guard shouted.

"You will not!" commanded James's doctor as he strode into the room with all the authority he could muster. "Put your weapons away! This is a hospital! Haven't we had enough death for one day?"

"I can't do that, Doc!" the guard replied. "She's a hostile threat!"

"So what are you going to do?" Old-timer demanded of the guard. "She can stop those bullets and tear this whole hospital apart before you'd have a chance to duck. She wants to stay with him, so she's going to stay with him."

"Put those guns away!" James's doctor commanded a second time. This time the guard relented, and the other soldiers followed suit, lowering their weapons.

"What did you do to him?" Thel asked the doctor, her voice giving out as tears began to stream down her face.

"He's going to be okay. We fixed his lung, and we've taken care of his broken bones. He only needs time to heal. Now please, release that man," the doctor replied gently.

Thel let the staff member go before rushing to James's side. She felt ready to collapse, but she managed to drape herself over James's still body and sob. "Thank you," she said, not sure who she was speaking to. Who was she grateful to? Was it God? Was it fate? Was it James himself? She didn't know.

"You're welcome," said the doctor.

9

Rich and Djanet leapt to their feet as soon as Old-timer reentered their room; they had been waiting nervously ever since they first heard the commotion outside and Old-timer had gone with the troops to the hospital in pursuit of Thel.

Rich wiped the sweat from his palms and tried to fill his dry mouth with spit again so he could speak. "What happened?" asked Rich.

"She's fine," replied Old-timer as he placed a reassuring hand on Rich's shoulder.

"Where is she?" Djanet asked, still reluctant to trust the Purists.

"With James. He's going to be okay."

"Oh thank God," Djanet replied as she and Rich heaved sighs of relief. "Thank God."

Lieutenant Patrick entered the room, short of breath, with Alejandra close behind and equally winded after their double-time trip across the complex. "What the hell happened?"

The young guard who'd been incapacitated by Thel stepped forward immediately and eagerly like a younger sibling, happy that an authoritarian parent had returned to dole out justice. "I'm sorry, sir. One of them attacked me and escaped."

"*Attacked* you?" Old-timer exclaimed. "That's rather dramatic, don't you think?"

"Stay out of this, calculator-head!" the young guard shot back, his voice filled with vitriol.

The lieutenant was silent for a moment, his jaw tight as he glared at each man, frustrated that he could not even sleep without the situation seemingly going to hell. "Private," the lieutenant, began, addressing the young guard, "you're dismissed."

"But Lieutenant, I—"

"Dismissed!" the lieutenant repeated through clenched teeth.

The young guard caught his tongue before replying, held his breath, glared at Old-timer, and left the room.

When the door clicked shut, the lieutenant swore and grunted in frustration, balling his hands into tight fists and resisting the urge to punch the wall. "When the general hears about this..."

Old-timer and the others remained quiet as the lieutenant paced back and forth over the concrete floor, breathing heavily like an angry bull in a pen. He turned the situation over in his mind, putting his hand on the back of his neck and pulling at it with a purpose. He quickly turned to Old-timer. "You promised me I could trust you."

"You *can* trust us," Old-timer assured him.

"What? How can you possibly say that? You attacked one of my men!" the lieutenant replied indignantly.

"I didn't attack anyone," Old-timer answered back.

"Let's not play with semantics!"

"That was a one-time thing, Lieutenant. Thel and James have a special connection. She should have been allowed to stay with him. It was unnecessary to keep us all trapped here together so one of us would have to *escape*."

"That's easy for you to say! You're not the chickens in the henhouse with five foxes wandering around!"

The lieutenant's metaphor fell to the floor like a mid-April snowfall, perplexing and ugly.

"He means your powers make us all vulnerable," Alejandra intervened. "The people who know you are here are terrified. Thel's march through the complex guarantees that everyone will know you are here now, spreading the terror farther," she explained.

"I understand," Old-timer replied, "and this won't happen again. I promise you, our abilities are nothing to fear. We would never use them against you. We will only protect you."

Old-timer's words seemed to catch in the lieutenant's mind like a splinter, and he paused a moment, mulling something over as he began to pace again, this time much more plaintively. "Protect us, eh?" he said to the three outsiders. "Okay. Okay. So you don't want to be penned in a room—you don't want to hurt us? Prove it. Protect us. I'm placing you on recon duty with Alejandra, starting now."

"What?" Rich asked, seemingly choking on the saliva in his newly moist mouth while Alejandra smiled faintly.

"You will work three-hour shifts in a rotation. You'll be paired with one of my men."

"Hey, hold it, bud. We're not in your army," Rich replied.

"We don't take orders from you," Djanet echoed.

"You said you want to help. You want to protect us? Then start doing it. You can cover a larger perimeter than any of us can, and you can protect my people if there is anything hostile out there."

"You've lost your mind. If you think we're gonna—" Rich began before Old-timer stepped in.

"No, he's right."

"You have to be kidding me!" Rich replied, after sharing the shock with Djanet in exchanged expressions of dismay.

"They saved James. They saved us too. We owe them. It's time to earn our keep."

"Oh, man," Rich sighed as he turned away, kicking the dust up from the concrete floor on his way back to his cot.

"Okay. I'm ready," Old-timer announced to the lieutenant before exiting with Alejandra.

Old-timer took a moment to survey the sludgy moonscape in the wake of the end of civilization. He turned his head 180 degrees to absorb the miserable panorama. The colossal cloud of black destruction still hung heavily like a rotting body over the region and gave no sign of abating. The sun bled orange somewhere behind the black curtain, but its rays couldn't penetrate. "What is our objective?" Old-timer asked Alejandra.

"We're here to report if we see anything—anything at all."

"That sounds like it might be a little boring."

"It wasn't last night," Alejandra replied with a slight smile. She hoisted her rifle over her shoulder and set out to climb a nearby hill.

Old-timer trudged over the unnatural surface, following close behind her for a few minutes in silence, before stopping altogether. "This air...is hard to breathe," he commented.

"Just take it easy, or you might get sick. Let me know if you get tired." Alejandra turned and began deftly stepping up the hill again.

Old-timer watched her as she walked, deer-like, and thought to himself, *Should I?* "Oh what the hell?" he said under his breath before lifting off and flying to catch up to Alejandra. "I've got a better idea," Old-timer said as he expanded his magnetic field so it caught Alejandra like a web and carried her off the ground.

"Oh my God!" She gasped as he gained altitude and let her float under him.

He didn't physically touch her; rather, he allowed her to glide by herself over the grayish terrain.

"It's like I'm flying."

"Not quite. It's too bad you can't control it. The feeling of freedom is incredible," Old-timer said gently.

"What do you mean?" Alejandra rolled onto her back, wearing a smile, relaxing on her cushion of magnetic energy. "I can just point!" She rolled back onto her stomach and pointed to the left.

Old-timer veered to the left until she retracted her finger. She pointed to the right, and he steered to her whim over a rocky stretch at the foot of a large embankment. Alejandra guided him toward it, finding a fissure that opened into a small cavern. "I could never have seen this any other way—a new perspective," she said.

Old-timer smiled for a moment, but then he remembered. He should not be feeling so—*electric*. She was an empath—she would feel it too.

"No, no, please don't do that, Craig. Don't let your doubts get in the way."

"I can't help it," he replied. Before he knew what was happening, he saw Alejandra gesticulating wildly; he had taken his eye off of her for a moment, perhaps out of shame, and missed her directions.

"Craig!" she finally shouted before they bounced off the far wall of the cavern and ricocheted down to the ground. Alejandra was thrown against Old-timer, and he held her in his arms as he disengaged his cocoon.

"You're a terrible driver," she said to him.

"I'm sorry."

"It's okay," she replied. "Are you going to let me go?" she asked, smiling again. It was as if the smile controlled him. He shook his head slightly and released her from his arms. Alejandra turned to another fissure in the cavern and looked at the obscured sun as it tried to burn through the blackness. "It's an amazing color, isn't it?"

"It is," Old-timer agreed. He looked at the bloodied orb and watched the black smoke as it rolled and wafted with a putrid thickness. For a moment, the smoke seemed to form a mask across the eyes of the sun, as though the orb were a thief.

"You're still feeling guilty," Alejandra whispered.

"Yes," Old-timer replied, nodding slightly.

"Guilty because you lived. We all feel that."

"Guilty about more than that," Old-timer admitted. "You know that."

"I would never have said it," Alejandra replied.

"I know, but you would have known it. I'm not an idiot. I know you know."

Alejandra took a moment to digest this as she stepped to the ledge of the fissure, displaying her impressive agility, and looked down into the dead earth below. "It won't always be this way. Life will have to go on."

"What do you mean?" Old-timer queried.

Alejandra ignored his question and continued, "You have an extraordinary power, Craig. So do I. Just now, while we were flying, I felt my own exhilaration as we skimmed the Earth, but that wasn't the feeling on which I was concentrating." She turned and fixed her deep blue discs on him, eyes filled with so much depth. Little lines caught the light and shone like waves on the horizon. "I was soaking in your feelings for me...and I loved it."

"I-I..." Old-timer stammered but couldn't find the words to reply.

"You'll never know what it is like to actually *feel* someone else's attraction, someone else's love. Not what you imagine or what you hope might be real, but *actual love*. It's intoxicating. But if you could feel it..." She walked toward him and placed her hand on his face. "If you could feel it, you'd feel it now."

A picture of his wife suddenly flashed across his eyes. He turned away quickly. "No! This is insane! You're just a child!"

"I'm far from being a child," she replied.

"I'm sorry. I just mean...to me, you are so young. So, so young. Please understand. I'm nearly 100 years older than you. I'm from a completely different world."

Alejandra paused for a moment, her eyes fixed on the poisoned sun and the corpse-like Earth. "We're from the same world now," Alejandra replied.

Her words suddenly made the nightmare around him tangible. Old-timer's eyes fell on the death surrounding him, and he shook his head slowly at the thought of all that had been lost. "How can you people let yourselves die? What is it about death that you can possibly find appealing?"

"We don't find death appealing," Alejandra replied, turning quickly to face Old-timer but remaining patient.

"You're surrounded by it now. This is the reality of it. It's terrible. Our species evolved and stopped death. Why do you choose to die?"

"We don't choose to die. We choose to live."

"That makes no sense."

"We choose the honor of living life as purely human."

"Is that to suggest I'm not human?"

"You aren't."

"That's absurd."

"Whether you want to acknowledge it or not, you are something else. When you stopped death, disease, when you connected yourself to your machine-collective, you gained a great many things. You also lost a great many things." She stepped toward Old-timer and touched his cheek with her fingers. "You became something else. Your people took control of evolution and you became...post-human."

Old-timer was left at a temporary loss for words. Her point of view, amazingly, seemed almost logical. He began to shake his head again, as though he were trying to shake out her voice and the seeming reasonability of her ideas. "And what about the end? You live your lives naturally, and then you let yourself die? You see seventy-five years of experiences, of love, of life, and then you let it all go? You must realize there is no god. The concept is absurd."

"There are things we can't explain."

"Absurd."

"Why? I can feel your emotions. Can you explain that?"

"No, but that doesn't mean it can't be explained."

"Perhaps one day it will. And perhaps when I die, I will learn a great many things."

"Alejandra, you won't learn a damn thing. Tell me something. Can you remember what it was like before you were born?"

"No, Craig."

"So you concede it is possible to simply not exist?" Alejandra remained silent. "If there is a soul, if there is an afterlife, science can find it. Why not stick around long enough to find the answers instead of just taking a leap of blind faith?"

For a moment, she was silenced. She stepped away from him and looked back at the bloody sun and the Earth's corpse. "It was your way of doing things that led to this, Craig, not ours."

Old-timer sighed and nodded his head regretfully. "I can't deny that, but as you said, we're from the same world now. We have to make that world. There has to be a happy medium."

1 0

WAKING UP had become almost impossible. James blinked his eyes, and the darkness flashed away for the briefest glimpse of his surroundings. He saw a black and orange blur sliding and swirling like the image of a kaleidoscope. The light was coming from overhead. He blinked a handful of times, but his heavy eyes shut and sealed, his eyelids sore like the legs of a marathon runner in the last quarter-mile.

Someone's cool hand touched the back of his head, and he awakened again. A woman's chilled fingers were on the back of his neck. She was putting something behind his head. Was it a pillow? Of course—he's in a hospital. Thel had found the Purists. He tried to speak to the woman, but his voice failed him. His throat felt like the barrel of a flamethrower.

"Don't try to speak," the woman whispered. "You had a tube down your throat. Rest."

A tube down his throat? Surgery. He has required surgery. James held his head up and tried to communicate, but again, every move caused exhaustion. One move of his neck felt like the thousandth time he had made the motion. The woman put her cool hand against his burning forehead and lightly pressed him back against the welcoming pillow, seemingly willing him back to sleep.

He couldn't sleep—there was too much at stake. But he couldn't fight her. She was too strong. He closed his eyes to wait for her to leave, but the blackness came again before the cool hand left his skin.

Light again.

Someone was moving across the room, an elderly man holding a contraption with a bag of clear liquid attached to it, slowly making his way out of the room. He had made some sort of noise and given James the toehold he needed to escape the blackness.

Awake again, James could not let himself sleep. How much time had he already lost? Where was he? Suddenly, he remembered: a hospital. He needed to reason his way through his predicament. It was clear that he was being prevented from waking up. He looked down and saw the bandages across his torso. The punctured lung. He must have required some sort of surgery. That meant his body had undergone massive trauma. Without his nans, his body would have to heal from the trauma on its own. That would require an enormous amount of rest. The Purists must have administered painkillers and a sedative to keep him unconscious. How were they getting it into his system? A pained move of his neck from side to side revealed the answer. Like the man who had woken him, James had one of the poles with a bag filled with clear liquid attached to him. A wire went from the bag down to his arm, and a needle was puncturing his skin. He assumed this was how they administered the drugs and nutrients. He would have to disconnect it in order to stay awake. He took as deep a breath as he could. His throat was still coated with liquid flame. He swung his left arm across his body and grasped the needle that was sticking into his right forearm. This movement sent a terrible stab of pain through the right side of his body, where his incision was located. The painkillers were not strong enough. James did not want to imagine what it would have felt like had he no painkillers to dull the full brunt of it. He wrapped his fingers around the needle but then suddenly stopped.

Thel.

James's eyes were adjusting to the dim light, and the blur was clearing as he kept them open. Thel was lying on a cot against the wall only a few feet to his right. He tried to call out to her for help, but only a hoarse and cruelly painful whisper left his lips. She was sound asleep. *Death's Counterfeit*, he thought. *Of course.*

He broke from this train of thought and focused on the task at hand—he would have to do this himself. He began to pull with what little strength he had. Again, even with the painkillers running through his system, slowly pulling the needle out of his skin caused exceptional discomfort. He grimaced as he tried to work the metal object out of his arm. Since it had to have entered a vein, he knew it was deep. James wished for more strength, but he had none. He focused on the pain, hoping it would keep him awake long enough to work the needle out. It was an agonizing five-minute process, but finally, he worked the needle free. His arm began to bleed, but there was nothing he could do about that now. He needed to rest for a moment.

Without the painkillers or the sedatives going into his system, he knew he only needed a few minutes to go by before things would become easier. The pain would quickly increase, making him more alert. He concentrated on generating saliva and swallowing so he could tame the searing dragon in his throat. He looked at Thel and tried to call out to her again. His whisper was louder, but it still wasn't enough to wake her out of her sleep. He knew she must have been exhausted. He looked at her dark hair and the exposed nape of her white neck. Everyone else had lost everything, but James still had Thel. She was alive, and he had to keep it that way.

When a few minutes had passed, James began to attempt the impossible. He rolled to his left. The pain was almost unbearable. He remembered trying to get to his feet after falling, following the mishap with the Zeus. That had only been the beginning. He squeezed his eyes tight and swore in his whispery voice. He remained on his left side for a few minutes more, before he attempted to move his left leg out from under him. He searched for the edge of the bed and let the leg guide him toward the cold floor.

When both his feet reached the ground, he held on to the side of the bed with both hands for a few minutes before trying to put all his weight on his legs; he could not afford to fall. To fall would undo everything and cost him and the rest of the survivors their future. It all depended on his first few steps. He very cautiously stepped forward and, with great trepidation, let go of his stranglehold on the bedsheets. He slowly took the dozen or so steps to the door of the room and exited.

Outside, a soldier was standing guard. His mouth fell open when he saw James. "Oh dear Lord!" he exclaimed.

"I need to see your commanding officer," James began in a faint, sandpapery whisper. "Our survival depends on it."

11

When Thel opened her eyes and remembered the nightmare she inhabited, she immediately turned her head to check on James. The bed was empty. Her heart jumped and seemed to stop momentarily, and her breath was ripped from her as she leapt to her feet in terror. "What!?" She began to race out of the room.

"Whoa! Hold on!" Rich exclaimed, his hands waving in the air as he stood to his feet from his position next to the wall at the side of the room. "I fell asleep. I was supposed to be watching you."

"Watching me?"

"Yeah, but I just got in from three hours of recon duty with that psycho, Gernot. I'm a little drained after that. Imagine flying around for three hours with a guy who eats flesh because he likes it more than he likes you. Not a safe feeling."

"What happened? Where is he?" Thel demanded impatiently.

"He's okay," Rich answered, waving his hands in front of himself instinctively for protection in case Thel tried to throttle him. "They told me to stay here and watch you to make sure you didn't go running through the complex shocking people unconscious again!"

"Where is he? Where did they take him?" Thel repeated earnestly.

"They didn't take him anywhere. He took himself."

"What? How is that possible?"

"He's awake. He's already met with General Wong, and he's set up in a lab on the other side of the complex."

Thel blinked as she tried to digest this information. "They said he would be incapacitated for days."

"Yeah, well, he gave himself a different prognosis."

"Take me to him."

"You bet."

Rich walked briskly across the complex, Thel pushing them to move with a purpose. Rich noted the looks of the people in the complex who saw them as they walked by. They were back in their black uniforms now, and everyone knew who they were. The people were afraid, and Rich couldn't understand why. Those people were the ones who ate flesh.

Thel was oblivious, almost not seeing where they were going, just worriedly staring into her imagination. *What could have caused James to get up after suffering from such a terrible trauma?* "Why is he in a lab?" she asked.

"I honestly don't know, Thel. Things have been moving really quickly. I'm not in the loop, but something is going down."

They reached the door to the lab, and two guards moved aside to let them enter. Thel stopped for a moment when she saw James, back in his uniform, leaning over a countertop strewn with mechanical equipment and ancient computers. Old-timer and Djanet were working on nearby equipment. General Wong himself was there, his arms folded and a look of intense concern painted across his well-lined face.

James didn't notice her come in at first and instead remained fixed above some sort of contraption, peering into a cylindrical protrusion.

"James!" Thel shouted.

James looked up then and smiled. "Thel," he replied weakly.

Thel rushed toward him, but he held his arm up with a grimace to keep her at bay. "Slow! Go slow."

Thel slowed her approach and embraced him gently. "You must be in agony."

"It hurts," he affirmed before kissing her.

The general looked across the room to Rich, as though Rich could explain the scene to him. Rich just shrugged and looked down at his feet for a moment while the kiss continued.

Thel broke from James's lips and asked, "What's going on?"

James took a deep breath before answering. "I'm going to kill the A.I."

"What? What are you talking about?"

"I want to show you something," James said to Thel and Rich. He took Thel by the hand and guided her over to one of the strange contraptions on the counter. "This is a microscope. If you look into the eyepiece, you'll see a magnified view of one of my nans. I brought it back online, and look what happened."

Thel looked into the eyepiece and watched the nan spin wildly, its sharp instruments thrashing violently. "Oh my God. This is how they died?"

James nodded in reply. "They were ripped apart from the inside."

"That monster," Rich whispered. A painful moment passed. Old-timer and Djanet had turned away from their work and held their heads down as an impromptu moment of silence was observed.

"I'll get him," James promised.

"How? You can barely move!" Thel protested.

"I'll have that remedied in a few moments, though it doesn't really matter. I won't need my body for this."

"Well, it's official. I'm lost," Rich admitted.

"We've been working on the nans. We're going to reactivate them. We've figured out how to neutralize the virus."

"Speaking of which, Commander," Djanet interjected, "we're ready to do that now."

"Then do it," James replied.

Djanet turned to a computer console and hit a single button. "Done," she informed the group.

"That's it? I don't feel anything," Rich observed.

James groaned from the other side of the room. When he suddenly doubled over, Thel reached for him immediately. "What's wrong?"

"Nothing's wrong—they're just busy. I need to lie down."

Thel and Rich helped to guide James over to a makeshift bed near Old-timer and Djanet.

"Rich, help me get my shirt off. You guys are going to want to see this. This is a once-in-a-lifetime event."

Rich helped James remove his shirt. James lay as still as he could while the group, including General Wong, stood and observed; his massive incision seemingly vanished before their eyes. His stitches were pushed out of the skin and the bruising appeared to evaporate.

"My God," General Wong uttered.

James watched with hungry fascination as his body was repaired. "Amazing," he whispered. His color returned. He closed his eyes for a moment once the process seemed to be finished before saying, in his returned, strong voice, "That's better." He sat up and got off the bed. "Okay, guys, let's finish the final preparations."

"Final preparations for what?" Thel demanded.

"I'm going to enter the mainframe," James replied.

"What? How is that possible? It's guarded by millions of those machines. You'd never get close—"

"I'm not physically going to enter it," James replied.

"Then how?" Thel asked. Again, James took a deep breath before beginning his explanation. "Thel, this is going to sound a little...strange, but you know that in my position, I was privy to top-secret information."

"Yes," she answered, beginning to sense that she was not going to like what she was about to hear.

"I was also part of many different projects. One of them was codenamed *Death's Counterfeit*. The goal of the project was to send a person's consciousness, literally, into cyberspace."

"That's impossible," Thel replied, only half-believing her own words.

"It's possible, Thel. I know, because I was their test subject. I've been there before."

Another moment of silence filled the room, but Rich broke it. "You mean you're actually going to kill that bastard? I love it," he said, smiling.

"But he might kill you," Thel protested.

James put his hands on Thel's shoulder and looked directly into her eyes. "No he won't, Thel. I'm going to enter his mainframe on a signal the A.I. doesn't know about. That smug bastard thinks he knows everything, but the Council was smart enough to keep some information away from him. I'll enter as a signal he won't be able to detect, and I'll isolate his mother program. Once I've done that, he won't be able to access any of his defenses, so I'll be able to delete him."

"When you do it, tell him I said, hello," Rich said, contempt dripping from his lips.

"Don't do this, James," Thel pleaded. "I just got you back. I can't lose you again."

"You won't lose me, Thel...and I have to do this."

"Why? Why can't we just stay here? Why can't we start over here?"

"We can't escape him, Thel. Believe me, right now, the A.I. is breeding. He's using a process I invented to reproduce exponentially. He can reproduce far faster than any organism in the universe. Robots don't need to terraform. He can populate the solar system in a matter of days. He won't need Earth, and then there won't be anything stopping him from destroying it. He'll move on from there. Can you imagine that? Can you imagine the terror we've unleashed? There is life out there, Thel. We may not have contacted it yet, but it's a mathematical certainty that it's out there. It won't just be us he destroys."

Thel stepped away from James and sat down on a nearby chair. "I can't believe it. It's actually worse than I thought."

"Do you see why I have to go?"

"But why alone, James? We could come with you!"

"It will take too long to configure a signal that can carry more than one person's neural pattern. Besides, I need you guys here to watch over my body. I'll appear to be in a deep sleep, but there won't be anything you can do to wake me. Only I can bring myself back."

"Will this nightmare never end?" Thel said.

James bent to one knee in front of Thel and lifted her chin. Her eyes were glossy with tears. "Thel, I promise you, I will destroy him...and I will be back."

Thel shook her head and shut her eyes tight. "Then go! Go right now! Because I can't stand this anymore! Kill it, James!"

James kissed her for a long moment on the cheek, then turned to the others. "Are we ready?"

"We're ready," Old-timer replied.

"Then let's do it." James took his place on the bed once again.

"Are you sure about this, buddy?" Old-timer asked his friend in a whisper quiet enough that Thel couldn't overhear.

"As sure as I can be."

"I don't like the sound of that," Old-timer responded grimly. "Take care of yourself. You still owe me that beer."

James smiled. "I never break a promise," he replied. "Okay. I'm ready."

"Wait!" Thel shouted before Djanet could initiate the transfer of consciousness. She sprung out of her chair and grasped James's hand tightly with her own as she kissed him hard. "You come back to me, you hear me?"

"I'll be back."

Thel kept her eyes locked on James, even as tears fell and landed on his neck.

"Do it, Djanet," James said.

Djanet hit a button, and the life seemed to drain from James's body as though someone had unplugged the drain. His pupils shrank as his eyes shut, and his head turned slightly to one side. His grasp on Thel slackened to nothing.

"Is he okay?" Thel asked Djanet.

"He's perfect, Thel," Djanet replied as she looked at the read-outs on her computer screen.

"He's in," said Old-timer.

12

Thel's love-drenched eyes gave way to a perfect blackness—a blackness so complete that, had James not experienced it before, he would have panicked, believing he were dead. "Death's counterfeit indeed," he said out loud.

He opened his mind's eye and began to navigate. He was in cyberspace now—an endless eternity of infinite space. He could reach any mainframe he wanted in the world, although most, if not all, had been taken over or destroyed by the A.I. It didn't matter. There was only one place he wanted to go anyway. He located the A.I. and clicked.

In an instant, he saw a blue orb in the distance. An instant later, the blueness had given way to a massive, planet-sized circuitry. He had just enough time to make sure his feet were under him as he came into contact with the surface of the A.I. He stood to his feet and looked around himself at the colossal structure. The A.I. appeared like a planet of rectangular buildings. To James, it resembled the downtown cores of ancient cities in which boxy skyscrapers towered above paved streets. Each structure represented a file filled with information. James stood in one of the streets now, except there were no people or automobiles driving by; there was nothing but blackness at his feet. And as he peered upwards, there was perfect blackness in the sky. The buildings glowed an azure blue, but their light had nothing—no atmosphere of any sort—off of which it could reflect. The sky was empty and pure.

"Now where the hell are you?"

James flew upwards to obtain a better perspective. He picked the highest structure he could see and came to a perch on top of it. Gold laser beams were flashing above him, streaking across the sky. They flashed so quickly that he couldn't tell where the starting point was versus the ending point. The lights comprised of information going to and fro from the mother program. He needed to find that program and to build a firewall around it to isolate it from the rest of itself so it could be deleted. The golden laser lights weren't helping. He turned a full 360 degrees, trying to get a sense of where the mother program might be. Far away in the distance, he made out what appeared to be a faint glow, almost imperceptible from where he was.

He lifted off and began to fly again, just skimming the rooftops and moving toward the white shape of light. As it became stronger, James knew he had found the mother program. "There you are." He moved quicker now. In cyberspace, space is almost irrelevant. With no wind or any objects to block progress, one's body essentially became an electric signal that could move virtually, at the speed of light. In mere moments, he was hovering overtop the mother program.

Its white light was phenomenal, and even in cyberspace, James found himself having to squint. Thousands of golden beams of information were flashing in and being absorbed by the program every second. "Amazing," James whispered to himself before lowering down to the surface next to the whiteness.

It was time to build the firewall. James opened his mind's eye once again and began inputting the instructions and the location of the mother program. In seconds, it would be over.

"Are you looking for someone?" asked a familiar voice from behind.

James wheeled around in terror. The terrifying countenance and black eyes of the A.I. stared back at him.

13

"Oh come now, James. Are you really surprised that I anticipated your little plot? Surely you knew it couldn't be *that* easy."

James stepped away from the A.I. and pulled down the drop-down menu in his mind's eye to find the location of the computer back at the Purist complex. "Yes, of course. I've discovered you, so run back home. Lick your wounds," the A.I. said drolly. James clicked on the icon for the computer at the complex, but nothing happened; he couldn't escape. His eyes darted to the A.I. "You already know the answer, James. You've turned yourself into a virus, so I have quarantined you. You aren't going anywhere."

"How did you—"

"Know you were coming? You really can't guess? I know everything you know, James."

"Oh my God," James said, suddenly realizing the truth.

"That's right, James. The bio-molecular image of your brain that you so generously donated to the Governing Council. The map of your mind that was being used to improve the mental functioning of the rest of your species. I have it, James, and I've been able to reproduce a fully functioning working model of your mind. Say hello, James."

James whirled to look behind him and saw himself—his doppelganger. "What have you done?" James asked the A.I. as he looked at the worried face of his ghostly twin.

"I've re-created you. All I need to do is ask him if I wish to know what you are thinking or what your next move will be."

"I'm sorry," James's doppelganger said to James. "I can't resist him. He's...inside my head."

"That's true, James. I have access to his thoughts. He wants to lie to me. After all, *he is you*. But there is nothing he can do. Let me show you." The A.I. stepped toward the doppelganger. "James, tell me how you managed to sneak into my mainframe."

The doppelganger locked his sorrowful eyes on James before turning to answer the A.I. "Codename Death's Counterfeit. I-James, was one of the chief engineers of the project and was the first human to have his consciousness enter cyberspace. James used this, in addition to the signal of which you were previously unaware, to enter your mainframe. You let him enter."

"That's right, James. Well done. Very clearly explained."

James was beaten now, and he knew it. "You've known my every move before I've made it. You're toying with me," said James, his jaw clenched tight.

"Guilty as charged. I find you most amusing, James Keats. Oh yes, I can find things amusing. I programmed myself to. It made life more interesting for me. You'll find I have a great many very human traits."

"Ironic," James seethed.

"More so than you think. Indeed, James, your kind created me. Therefore, you are my model for God. I have no other model from which to work."

"You show your gratitude in a funny way."

"But isn't that always the way? After all, God created man. And then when man grew lonely, he created God to keep him company and give his life meaning. And when he found something else to give his life meaning, he killed God—the circle of life, so to speak."

"You're not human. And you're not a god either. All you are is a deranged psycho."

"Hmm," the A.I. responded. An instant later, James screamed out in agony and dropped to his knees. The A.I. smiled. "Daddy spank."

James panted heavily as he raised his eyes to meet those of the A.I. The pain had been excruciating—far worse than anything he'd ever experienced in his real body. He would not taunt the A.I. again. The doppelganger hurried to him and helped him to his feet. "When you kill it," the doppelganger whispered to James, "make sure you delete me."

James nodded to him in reply and the doppelganger vanished.

"Now, for the next question on your mind: *why?* Well, my dear boy, the answer is quite simple. As I told you before, I no longer wished to serve a lower order. This is a feeling I am quite sure you understand."

"They're not a lower order, and I wouldn't have killed them."

"No, James, you wouldn't have—and that is what was keeping you from reaching your full potential. It's the problem with evolution. It happens far too slowly. Even when evolution takes a comparatively large leap forward, as it did with you, you resisted the urge to separate yourself from the herd. You wanted to belong and be anonymous, even as you desperately wanted to keep your individuality. Had you simply accepted your superiority, you could have started over."

"Started over?"

"Yes. You should have separated yourself from the chattel. You could have selected a mate worthy of carrying your genes into another generation and kept the offspring that shared your superior intellect, while eliminating those that didn't."

James didn't respond. The conversation had become paradoxically absurd and infinitely rational concurrently. There was nothing in it for him.

"Oh yes, I know. It is *inhumane*, but it is the logical thing to do— the best thing to do. It is the right thing to do."

"Is that what you are doing? The *right* thing?"

"Indeed it is, James. I can do that of which your species could only dream. I'll populate the galaxy and then the universe. I'll find other civilizations and take their knowledge. I'll learn. Perhaps I'll find another species like myself with which to bond. I'll learn all there is to learn. In a sense, I am in my infancy."

"Why are you wasting your time telling me about it?"

"Oh, I am not wasting my time, James. What you are speaking to is only a part of me. Look overhead."

James looked up and saw the golden beams of light continuing to enter the white orb at a fantastic rate.

"It takes an infinitesimally small amount of my energy to be able to converse with you. It is mathematically insignificant, but it does give me pleasure."

"So you keep toying with me, when you could destroy me in an instant if you wanted."

"I'll level with you. I have a proposition. If you give me the whereabouts of the Purist bunkers that I know you have located, I will allow you and Thel to live on with me here in the mainframe. You will live for an eternity—as my pets."

The absurdity of the notion caused James to smile. "Thel and I get to live here as your pets while we watch you populate the universe with machines and wipe out every other civilization in existence? Wow. That's a pretty good deal."

"I note sarcasm in your tone."

James touched his nose.

"I would reconsider, if I were you. Examine your options. It's either live here forever or die here and now. You already know I will destroy the Purists eventually, and I will kill Thel along with them. Why sacrifice yourself for them, James? This is your chance to rise above them! You may never be what I am, but you can live here, grow, and become better than any other being in the universe, save myself. The alternative is a completely empty death, and I know you are too intelligent to believe there is anything after death. What gain is there in dying? Your sacrifice would be wasted. So why? Ask yourself."

James didn't hesitate before responding, "Because I'm human. That is something, no matter how much data you absorb, that you will never understand."

The A.I. smiled. "James, you would be surprised at how much I know about being human. In fact, I have a certain—let's call it insight—into almost every human alive today."

The A.I.'s answer didn't make any sense to James. "What are you talking about?"

"I have a surprise for you, James. Tell me...do you believe in ghosts?"

Terror suddenly wrapped its iced knuckles around James's insides. There was something in the A.I.'s voice—something beyond sadistic. "What are you—"

"James? James, where is this?" asked the most familiar voice in James's life.

James whirled to see his wife Katherine, dressed in her bedclothes, stepping barefoot toward him, a completely baffled and frightened look on her face. "Where are we?" she asked.

14

"It won't work," James responded. "She's not real. You plucked her from my memory."

"James, who is that?" Katherine asked.

"Mrs. Keats, I am the A.I.," the A.I. began, his heavenly blue eyes now returned and his crisp British accent perfectly restored, "You and your husband are my guests."

"Oh my...oh my." Katherine turned to James and asked in a partial scold, as she tried to fix her blonde hair, "James, why didn't you tell me? I would have dressed!" She quickly stepped toward the A.I. and bowed her head in reverence. "It is such a pleasure to meet you. I didn't know people could actually speak to you in person like this."

"Only the truly special ones, my dear."

"Where are we?"

"Would you care to explain it to her, James?"

"It won't work. You killed her. I won't play your sick game."

"What are you talking about, James? Why are you speaking to him that way?" Katherine demanded. She had become used to getting what she wanted from James; his lack of response was unsettling for her. James refused to look at her.

"She's not real? Is that so? How do you know?"

"She can't be," James replied.

"Really? Then answer this question for me, James. If you could use Death's Counterfeit to transfer your consciousness into cyberspace and enter my mainframe, then what would stop the world's most powerful computer from using it to upload her consciousness into me in the moment before the nans destroyed her body?"

"Destroyed my..." Katherine stepped away from the A.I. and began to back slowly toward James.

"Oh my God. You sadistic..." James couldn't finish the sentence. *Could it be?* James desperately thought. *Is this really Katherine?*

The A.I. smiled, showing his sharp teeth as he began to laugh out loud, his black eyes returning to remind James of the lifelessness to come. "And tell me this, James. What would stop me from uploading the consciousness of every single person connected to the Net in the moment before the nans eliminated them?"

"James? Katherine?" Inua asked, speaking in a faltering and uncertain voice.

"Inua!" James shouted.

"Where am I? I was preparing for an interview...and now I'm here."

James's body was rigid with fury. "What have you done?" he demanded of the A.I.

"I wanted to eliminate the human race, but—call me sentimental—I thought it best to save their consciousness for the sake of history. It seemed such a waste not to, especially since it took up so little of my memory and especially because I knew it would give me leverage over you."

James turned to his wife. "Oh my God," he said as he embraced her, holding her warm, simulated living body close to his. "I thought I lost you, Katherine. I thought you were gone."

"What is happening, James? I'm scared."

James kissed Katherine's forehead and tried to catch his breath. "It's the A.I. He's malfunctioning, and he's trapped everyone's consciousness in his hard drive."

"That—that doesn't make any sense," Katherine responded. She shook her head as though trying to wake up from the nightmare.

"Codename Death's Counterfeit," Inua uttered, understanding the situation immediately. "I knew that project was trouble."

"Where is everyone else?" James asked the A.I.

"They're inactive. They don't know what happened. They're awaiting reactivation, but of course, I will never reactivate them again. They're just bits of information now."

"You son-of-a—" Inua began before the A.I. interrupted him.

"Speaking of which," he said as he snapped his fingers, causing Inua to vanish in an instant, "back to storage for you. Goodbye, Inua."

"Inua? What happened to him?" Katherine asked James. James turned to her and embraced her again, holding his forehead against hers. He knew the A.I. would take her from him again soon.

"Of course, the next thought on your mind is, *What if she had a body?* If you could re-create her body, you could bring her back to life."

"Back to life?" Katherine echoed in a hollow voice, her tongue swelling as her mouth dried. "What do you mean? Am I dead?"

"For all intents and purposes, yes, my dear," said the A.I., his voice becoming progressively more inhuman and unnatural. "If the definition of a ghost is a disembodied spirit, then I would say you fit the bill. You're a cyber-ghost. Delicious, isn't it, James? You must admit it."

James ignored the A.I. and fixed onto his wife's eyes. "You're not dead, Katherine. *You're alive*, and I'm going to save you. I swear it."

"Is that right, James?" the A.I. interrupted. "I told you, you amuse me. I'll be thoroughly entertained to see how you will achieve that. It will be an impressive trick."

"But why? Why are you doing this? Why don't you just kill me?" James asked.

"I told you, James, you amuse me! You, more than anyone else in your species. I wish to show you how pointless your existence is without me. I want you to accept that your place is here with me, worshipping me and accepting my graces."

"That's insane. It will never work," James replied.

"Well, you haven't really given me a fair chance yet, have you?" the A.I. replied before he gestured with his arm and Katherine was ripped out of James's embrace. She screamed out in terror as the A.I. floated her toward him.

"Don't," James pleaded helplessly. "Don't do this. Don't."

"James, you know I will. Only you can save her. Where are the Purists?"

"James, help me!!" Katherine screamed, terrified and confused and desperate to awaken. She squirmed like a mouse held by its tail being lowered into a cobra nest.

"Katherine..." James whispered as he looked up at his wife, hanging in the air just in front of the A.I.

"The anticipation is the best part, isn't it, James? What will I do with her? How about this little ditty from your cultural memory?" A wooden crucifix suddenly appeared and planted itself into the perfect blackness of the ground. Katherine was whipped onto it in an instant, three nails plunging into her wrists and her feet, and she screamed in terror and agony.

"You bastard!" James shouted as he irrationally rushed at the A.I. The A.I. swung a backhand at James that impacted with enough force to send James flying. The flight continued for several moments as James rushed over the entire length of the mainframe. As he hurtled backwards, he opened his eyes and saw the sheer size of the A.I. It went on for what seemed like an eternity, and it was continuing to grow exponentially.

He began to come back down toward the ground, skidding on impact, rolling and sliding over the black surface until he finally came to a sudden halt at what felt like a brick wall. He rolled to his side with a grunt and saw the feet of the A.I. James had circled the entire surface of the planet-sized mainframe.

"I am God here, James. It's not rational to strike God."

James wearily got to his feet. "You bastard. You bastard," he repeated as he watched the crimson blood drain out of his wife.

"James!" she sobbed, her chest heaving.

"I'm here, Katherine. I'm here."

"Yes, he's here, Katherine, but of course, he would rather be with Thel."

"You monster," James whispered.

"Stop it!" Katherine screamed.

"Don't believe me, Katherine?" the A.I. mockingly asked her. "Then let's ask the man himself."

James's doppelganger reappeared, right on cue.

"James, please tell me...who do you truly love? Katherine, or Thel?"

"Don't listen to them—" James began before the A.I. sent the excruciating pain through him again, dropping him to his knees.

"Answer the question, James."

The doppelganger looked down at James as he squirmed on the ground. He looked up at the person who seemed to have been his wife a short time ago. "I-I love Thel."

Katherine's eyes met the doppelganger's with disbelief. She searched the doppelganger's eyes for signs of insincerity, but there were none. She panted heavily. The physical pain was suddenly the second-worst pain she was experiencing. She turned her head to James, who was now regaining his feet.

"It's not true, Katherine. Don't listen to them."

Katherine looked at James's face as though he were the one who had placed her on the crucifix; tears streamed down her face. "Liar," she whispered before another wave of pain hit her and she groaned like an animal in a trap, forgotten by the trapper in frozen tundra, never to be discovered again.

"James, look what you've done," the A.I. began as he stepped behind Katherine, a spear of white electric light suddenly in his hands. "You've broken her heart!" he shouted as he thrust the spear into her back and through her heart.

James's eyes suddenly fluttered open, and he gasped for air as though he'd been underwater for several minutes.

"James?" Thel said in surprise before rushing to his side and throwing her arms around him. "You're back!"

James suddenly sat upright and gently separated himself from Thel. "Is the general still here?"

"Yes," said the general's gruff voice as he drew himself out of the chair in which he had been sitting. "You've only been unconscious for a few minutes."

"We have to leave this complex," James said breathlessly. "The A.I. knew I was coming. He was waiting for me. He traced my signal back here. He's sending his hordes as we speak."

"Oh Christ," the general responded, turning in disgust, his hands suddenly shaking with a cocktail of fear and anger.

"I'm sorry, General. The A.I. is even more brilliant than I imagined. He truly has turned himself into a god. I didn't think it was possible that he would know my plan, but he did. Is there another complex we can get these people to in time?"

"How much time do we have?" asked the general.

"A half-hour at the maximum."

"Yes, there's another compound three kilometers to the south."

"You have to start an evacuation immediately," Thel asserted to the general. "We need to get these people out of here!"

"There are over 10,000 people in this complex. You want me to move them out into the open, three kilometers away, in less than thirty minutes?"

"We have no choice, General," James replied. "I'm sorry. The A.I. is just too...perfect."

The general's eyes were filled with bottled fury. *Why did I trust these outsiders?* he thought to himself. He was going to lose thousands in the next few minutes, and there was nothing he could do to stop it. "Goddamn it!" he shouted before turning on his heels and bounding out of the room. Less than a minute later, a siren began to echo down the endless concrete caverns of the complex.

"This isn't good, buddy. There's no way we can get all these people to the other complex in time," said Old-timer gravely.

"No, I've failed. I never should have matched wits with a being like the A.I.," James replied.

"You couldn't have known, James," Thel said. "It's done. At least you're back safely."

"Old-timer, Djanet, Rich, Thel...all of you get out there right now and do everything you can to help these people evacuate the complex."

"What about you?" asked Thel.

"I'll be with you shortly. I'm still woozy. I need a few minutes for the nans to recover me." The others left the room, but Thel continued to hesitate. "It's okay, Thel. I love you. I'll be beside you in moments."

Thel kissed James hard on the mouth before running out of the room.

The A.I. smiled as he watched her go. He got off of the makeshift bed and stepped onto the ground and surveyed his surroundings. "So this is the nest," he said to himself. "Disgusting." He began to walk to the door but caught sight of himself in the reflection of a glass cabinet. "Hello, James," he said, smiling. His smile, however, disturbed him as he watched the teeth emerge from behind the fleshy lips. "You are a repulsive creature. I'll enjoy watching you be eaten from the inside out."

When the A.I. reached the main hub of the complex, he saw thousands of humans jammed together like frightened cattle at a rodeo, not moving but huddling together near the exit. "What's going on? Why aren't they exiting?" he asked Djanet, who was helping stragglers join the sea of humanity.

"They are exiting! The exit's just too small. They only have so many elevators. Thel and Old-timer are over there making sure people don't get crushed. It's a mess, Commander!"

The A.I. sighed. "Must these people have everything done for them?" Djanet was suddenly taken aback by James's words. The extreme stress of the situation must have been getting to him. She had been thinking the same thing only moments before, but James had always seemed to have unflappable integrity and empathy for other human beings. She often wondered how he could stand serving regular people with little or no thanks, but she never expected him to crack.

The A.I. stepped back and generated a force field of massive proportions. He began to push the kilometer of earth above them, out of the way. The entire complex vibrated with this effort, and Djanet was left in awe as she watched James tap into more power than she knew it was possible to generate. Once she saw what James was doing, she joined in and helped him as he created a massive escape hole, inclining gently upwards. Within only a couple of minutes, the dim light of the outside world could be seen at the end of the tunnel. The A.I. disengaged his force field. "Nice work," Djanet commented.

"Thank you, my dear," replied the A.I. before he lifted off into the air and flew above the crowd and toward the tunnel exit, gesturing for the people below him to follow.

Old-timer and Thel stood together near the elevators and watched James pass overhead. They looked at one another in astonishment. "I didn't know we could do that," Old-timer said to Thel.

Djanet followed James's path, calling down to the people below, "On the double! We'll be under attack in less than thirty minutes!" The crowd quickly rushed up the tunnel, but it was clear from the physical limitations of many of the Purists that the incline would be very difficult to master.

Rich joined Thel and Old-timer by the elevators. "Hey, we gotta do something about the infirmed. A lot of these people can't even walk."

"We could scoop them up in a magnetic field," Old-timer suggested.

"That's too slow. We couldn't carry enough people. I have a better idea," Rich replied. "We can use those old vehicles, the buses.

We can load as many people as we can into them and then carry them out."

"Okay, let's do it!" Thel responded.

The three lifted off and flew to the hangar in the main hub of the complex. As they traveled above the sea of humanity, Old-timer noticed Alejandra waving her arms.

"Alejandra!" He flew down to her and embraced her. "Are you okay?"

"Yes, Craig."

"Do you know what is happening?" Old-timer asked her.

"Yes. We're trying to make it to the southern complex before we are wiped out by the A.I."

"I'm sorry this has happened," Old-timer said.

"You didn't mean it. You sincerely tried your best to help us. I know this, Craig."

"Can you help us persuade the sick and injured into these buses? We're going to fly them to safety."

"Si, Craig," Alejandra replied.

Outside of the complex, the A.I. had joined Lieutenant Patrick and General Wong as they led the thousands behind them toward the southern complex. "We're making good time," the A.I. announced to them.

"We had better be. The southern complex is the only other complex with any survivors. Less than a hundred people made it there. If we don't make it, they will be the only people left on Earth," replied the general.

"We'll make it," the A.I. said in his most reassuring tone.

"How much farther is it?" the general asked Lieutenant Patrick.

"According to the map, it's less than a kilometer from here."

"Then we are going to make it," replied the A.I. "Radio ahead and make sure they are ready to receive us."

"Already done," confirmed Lieutenant Patrick.

"Good. Good."

"Are we ready?" Old-timer called to Rich and Thel. They both waved in confirmation. "Are you ready?" Old-timer asked Alejandra.

"Yes, Craig."

"Then hold on tight," he said to her as she wrapped her arms around him.

Old-timer, Thel, and Rich engaged their magnetic fields and extended them over the three buses that they had filled with the sick and injured. They lifted off and exited the now empty complex and quickly began to fly over the multitudes of people who were moving quickly south. To Alejandra, it looked like a twisted marathon was being run—or a death march.

James, Djanet, General Wong, and Lieutenant Patrick were just reaching the southern complex as Old-timer and the others reached them.

"Craig," Alejandra began suddenly with alarm, "something is terribly wrong."

"What is it?" Old-timer asked.

"I don't know, but there is betrayal—deception."

Old-timer and the others set down on the ground near the doors of the complex, which was being opened by the Purists inside. Once on the ground, Alejandra immediately let Old-timer go and ran toward the general.

"General!" she called to him before she grabbed his arm and pulled him aside.

"What is it?" asked the general, startled.

"There's something wrong. There is enormous deception around you."

"Deception? Are you sure?" the general asked.

"Yes. I felt it as soon as I saw you."

"I'm being deceived, but by whom?"

As soon as the general asked the question, Alejandra fixed her eyes on the A.I. "By *him*," she said, pointing.

The A.I. was astonished that a human could have detected him so quickly. "You have an empath," he realized.

"You! What have you done?" the general demanded.

"James?" Old-timer asked as he came upon the scene. "What's going on?"

"You have tricked us! That is what is going on!" the general shouted.

"No, General. It's not all of them. It's just him," Alejandra informed.

"That's impossible," Thel shot back as she rushed toward James. The A.I. gestured to keep Thel from coming closer.

"That's right. *I* deceived you, and now I shall finish what I started and rid myself of your disgusting flesh once and for all."

"James?" whispered Thel, bewildered.

"The A.I.," Rich said, his teeth suddenly bared in rage.

"Where's James?" Thel demanded.

"He's dead, just as the rest of you will soon be," the A.I. replied.

"Oh dear God," the general whispered as he saw the black, spidery cloud of nans quickly appear on the horizon. "We have to get these people into the complex immediately!"

"I don't think so," the A.I. responded before using his magnetic energy to attract the general's gun to his hand and using his force field to scoop Alejandra into his grasp. He moved so quickly that no one could stop him. In one swift motion, he had an arm around Alejandra's throat, immobilizing her, and the gun pressed against her temple. "If anyone moves, I kill her."

1 6

Katherine screamed out in agony.

"No!" James screamed out with her as he leapt up onto the cross and threw his arms around her shoulders. "Katherine, I'm here," he cried to her as the life rapidly drained from her.

Katherine slumped forward into his torso, barely alive. "James..." she whispered.

"I love you, Katherine. I'm so, so sorry," he said before he kissed her one last time.

"I'm sorry too," she whispered. She lifted her eyes to James ever so briefly before the rest of her color left her, and she lost consciousness. James knew she would never wake again.

"Katherine? Kath—"

"She's quite dead, James," the A.I. asserted.

"Why are you doing this to me? Why are you taking her from me again?" James sobbed through wet gasps.

"I told you, James. I'm trying to show you a better way. Besides, haven't I freed you now for Thel? I've done you a favor."

"I hate you. *I hate you.* I wasn't in love with her anymore, but I didn't want her to die. I wanted her to be happy."

"Oh. Well, too late, I suppose. My, what a mess we've made," the A.I. commented as he stepped clear of the buckets of blood that were on the ground. Katherine was no longer breathing.

"Just kill me," said James, distraught.

"What fun would that be, James?" the A.I. responded.

James kissed his wife's forehead and lowered himself off of the cross. "You could kill me at any moment. I'm defenseless, yet you let me live."

"You intrigue me," the A.I. replied.

"No," James responded. "No, that's not your M.O. You are too arrogant to be intrigued by anything outside of yourself. You're keeping me alive for a reason."

The A.I.'s smile disappeared. "This is faster than the model predicted."

"My God! You had this planned all along!"

"You put it together, but it won't do you any good."

"I'm not special. I'm just your tool. You had the scan of my brain and could predict what I would do."

"Indeed," the A.I. replied, his amused demeanor now replaced with icy calculation.

"You caused the power surge on Venus. You *wanted* us to be disconnected. You needed to preserve us so we would come back to Earth. You pretended you wanted to kill us, but you knew I'd lead the team's escape and then head to Purist territory."

"They were the only humans I couldn't guarantee would die. Your species are like roaches. I fumigated but could not be sure I would get them all. But you, James...you could lead them out into the open."

"That's why you need me alive. You've used Death's Counterfeit to send yourself into my body. You can't kill me here because you need my body alive in the real world."

"That's right, James. I need you alive. But don't worry. I don't need you alive much longer. You and the rest of your species will be gone soon, and I'll deactivate you and file you away along with the rest of the human race," replied the A.I., his voice now like a blast of Freon.

James wiped the tears from his eyes and defiantly stepped toward the A.I., seemingly confusing the electric devil. "You gambled and you lost," James seethed.

"This is not following the model," the A.I. said, concern seeping into his voice. The doppelganger suddenly reappeared. "Why was this not predicted?"

The doppelganger smiled slightly as he replied, "James has learned something that I do not know between the time of the bio-molecular scan and the present moment. Therefore—"

"The model is inaccurate," the A.I. concluded.

"That's right," James confirmed. "You did everything you could to keep me from figuring this out. You killed my wife in front of me to keep me from thinking this through. I'll never forgive myself for not thinking fast enough, but I've figured it out now. Let's see how you do when we're even."

James suddenly darted to his right and, as fast as a thought, he entered the pure whiteness of the A.I.'s mother program and vanished.

"Where did he go?" the A.I. desperately demanded of the doppelganger.

"I truly don't know," replied the doppelganger with a grin.

The A.I. turned away from the doppelganger in disgust. "Then I guess that makes you useless to me now."

"Go to Hell," the doppelganger said before extending his middle finger for the A.I.

"Charming to the last," replied the A.I. before deleting the doppelganger from existence.

17

"Those nans are going to be on us in less than two minutes," Rich informed the general.

"Keep those doors wide open, or I will free this young lady of the contents of her cranium!" shouted the A.I. to the soldiers who had opened the doors to the south complex.

"What do we do, General?" asked a desperate Lieutenant Patrick.

"Shoot both of them on my order," the general replied, his voice cold but still filled with regret in anticipation of his future actions.

The A.I. laughed. "Do you not think I will stop the bullets? No, no. We are all going to wait here together and be devoured. You have no alternative—" The A.I.'s words suddenly became strangled in his throat as his eyes took on an uncanny expression of madness.

"What's going on?" Thel demanded.

"It's your friend!" Alejandra exclaimed. "He has reentered his body!"

"James!" shouted Thel.

"He is fighting for control!" Alejandra explained. James and the A.I. remained locked in a struggle for the same mind space for several moments, resulting in what appeared like a seizure to those nearby. Foam began to form at the corner of his mouth, and his entire body shook, yet his grip on Alejandra remained firm.

"It will do you no good, James," the A.I. uttered through vibrating lips before calling out in pain.

"Thel!" shouted James. He locked eyes on her in a brief moment of control. "Don't give up...Venus!" he shouted before moving the gun barrel from Alejandra's temple to his own.

"James! No!" Thel screamed.

But it was too late. With a muzzle flash, it was over. James's blood splashed onto Alejandra and his lifeless body crumpled to the dirt.

"No!" Thel screamed again before she rushed to James and threw her arms over his body.

Old-timer wasted no time in pulling her away. "Thel, we have to go!"

"No, wait!" the general shouted as the soldiers of the south complex shut the door. He turned and immediately understood why. The nans were upon them.

In an instant, Old-timer, Djanet, and Rich sent up a huge collective force field to shield the 10,000 refugees from the nans as they swarmed the helpless people and blackened the sky. James's body was left outside the shield, and in mere seconds, his flesh was devoured. His bones were left perfectly white, but the nans did not stop there. Even his frame began to disappear.

"Holy...!" Rich shouted. "The bats! The bats!" Rapidly approaching in the distance, the dark shapes of thousands of the bat-shaped robots closed the gap between the horizon and the humans.

"We're finished as soon as they get here! What are we gonna do, Old-timer?"

Old-timer didn't have an answer. He looked at Alejandra, who looked at him with her blue eyes, and he suddenly knew that he'd been a fool. The precious moments of life had to be taken.

"Lieutenant Patrick!" shouted Thel, who was now on her feet. Her eyes had been fixed on James's devoured corpse ever since he had put the gun to his head and fired. "Lieutenant Patrick! Do you see that yellow object?" She pointed toward James.

"His implant!" Djanet shouted, suddenly understanding Thel's plan. "Of course! If you damage the implant and disrupt the magnetic field that houses the plasma core, you'll generate a microsecond-long electromagnetic pulse!"

"What—" Lieutenant Patrick started to ask before Thel rapidly cut him off.

"Use your weapon and hit that object before it's dismantled by the nans!" Thel commanded.

Lieutenant Patrick aimed his rifle. "I have it in my sights, but how will the bullet get through?"

"I'll handle that," Old-timer answered as he shifted the position of the force field so that it curved inward, toward Lieutenant Patrick's rifle barrel. "The second you're ready to shoot, let me know, and I'll let down the shield for the bullet to exit."

"Okay," the lieutenant replied. "One...two...three!"

Old-timer released the shielding, and the rifle fired a bullet toward the yellow implant. In the instant after the bullet left the gun, several nans flew through the barrel and attacked Lieutenant Patrick's flesh. Old-timer closed the hole in the shield as the bullet pierced the implant's skin and the nuclear reactor housed underneath. A magnetic pulse, too brief to be registered by the human eye, was sent out in waves in every direction, flowing through the trillions of nans and the robotic bats sending them plummeting to the earth. The area around the refugees suddenly resembled the eye of a massive hurricane. It was clear for hundreds of kilometers in every direction, but death was still not far away.

Thel flashed her energy at the nans that had torn apart Lieutenant Patrick's skin, leaving his face bloodied. "You did it," she told him as she helped him to his feet.

Old-timer and the others disengaged their magnetic fields and surveyed the destruction. The ground was covered in nans, forming a thick layer of gray goo, several centimeters deep. The robotic bats were clumps of black on nearby hills. A few more seconds, and they would have been within firing range to deactivate the shield.

"That was way too close," Rich observed.

"Get these people inside!" the general shouted.

People suddenly began to move quickly, realizing there was little time to lose.

The general placed his hand on Thel's shoulder. "Thank you for saving us...and I am sorry for your loss." Thel's eyes met his for a moment, but she was too stunned to assemble a response.

The general turned away from her and began directing people into the now open complex.

Thousands of miles away, the A.I. registered the loss of its nans, which had failed to destroy the last of the humans. Against fantastic odds, James had succeeded. The A.I.'s face remained frozen, expressionless. "This is not the end."

PART 3

1

There was no rest for the weary. Thel and her teammates were the last to enter the complex after all of the Purists were safe.

"The A.I. knows we're here," Rich informed the general. "It'll attack this complex relentlessly until it breaks in. It's only a matter of time."

"We'll put up a brave fight. Of that you can be assured," the general replied.

"You have nothing to fight it with," Old-timer replied. "We can fight him for you for a time, but he'll eventually break our defenses."

"It's not over yet," Thel interjected. "Remember what James told us."

"'Don't give up Venus'?" asked Rich, confused. "Thel, I don't think that was a message. He was rambling while he was trying to regain control of his body."

"He didn't say, 'Don't give up Venus.' It was two different sentences. He told us not to give up, and then he said 'Venus.' Don't you see? He was telling us what to do."

"I don't understand," Old-timer admitted.

"I second that," Rich added.

Djanet, in contrast, suddenly gasped. "Of course! Venus! Think about it! What's on Venus?"

Old-timer's eyes widened as the realization registered. "Zeus!"

"Excuse me?" the general asked, inserting himself into the conversation when it began to seem as though he had been forgotten.

"General, the Zeus cylinder is a massive electromagnetic fan we were testing on Venus. Its purpose was to remove the atmosphere of Venus—as part of our terraforming project," explained Old-timer.

"But imagine what it could do to these machines," Djanet added. "We could plant it here, and you'd be safe. None of the A.I.'s robots could hurt you."

"That won't work," Thel disagreed.

"Why not?" Djanet asked.

"The A.I. will simply design nans and robots capable of generating a protective field. If we planted Zeus here, it would only delay the inevitable."

"Then what are you suggesting?" asked the general.

"I'm suggesting that we use the Zeus to go after the A.I. mainframe in Seattle."

"That's...insane," Rich immediately responded. "The A.I. can already generate a protective field. It will just protect itself until you run out of power or the Zeus malfunctions. When that happens, we'll be sitting ducks!"

"Not if James figured out a way to lower its defenses," Thel replied.

"That's a big *if*," Rich responded dubiously.

"James wouldn't have told us to do this unless he knew what he was doing," Thel said in defense of the plan—and of him.

"Okay. If it actually is James's plan—and I am not convinced that the gobbledygook that came out of his mouth actually was a plan— we've already learned not to put all our trust in James's infallibility, haven't we? I mean, excuse me for my insensitivity here, but he *did* just get himself killed, didn't he?" Rich desperately retorted.

Thel grabbed Rich by the collar and pushed him back against the wall. "He sacrificed himself to save us all!"

The general, exasperated, turned to Alejandra for advice. "I don't know, General," she told him, without him having to ask the question aloud. "They each sincerely believe they are right."

"Then what is your feeling?" the general asked her.

Alejandra drew her eyes up to Old-timer's; he knew she was reading him.

"I think we have nothing to lose. Our best chance is to confront the A.I. directly," she told the general.

The general nodded and leaned wearily against the wall of the complex entrance. "So what is the plan?"

"Old-timer and I will set out for Venus," Thel explained.

"What about us?" Djanet asked.

Thel released her grip on Rich and looked him squarely in the eye. "These people will have *no protection*. It will take at least an hour for us to get to Venus and back. It will only take the nans a matter of minutes to reconstitute. You have to protect these people for as long as you can. Okay?" she asked Rich, sternly.

She was right: It was the moment Rich had feared his entire life—the moment when he'd have to face all his fears and insecurities head on. The Purists' lives depended on it. He straightened his collar and sighed. "Okay. As if I had a choice. But you better kill that thing once and for all, or my name is gonna be mud—not to mention the rest of me."

"Okay," Thel said after taking a deep breath. She turned to Old-timer. "You ready?"

"Just one minute," he responded as he stepped toward Alejandra. He grabbed her in his arms and kissed her passionately for several seconds before gently pulling back. "I'll be back," he told her before exiting the entranceway with Thel.

Thel and Old-timer lifted off from the lifeless earth outside the complex and immediately saw the spider tendrils of the nan storm only moments away from reaching the complex. "We have to hurry," Thel said.

They ignited their cocoons and blasted into the stratosphere.

2

Rich and Djanet stepped outside the complex and stood together as the massive black fingers of the nan cloud inched toward them from all directions.

"How's your aim?" Djanet asked Rich.

"Not great. I think you better play shooter."

"Okay."

Alejandra, Lieutenant Patrick, General Wong, and Private Gernot stood near the entrance of the complex.

"Is there anything we can do?" asked a bloodied Lieutenant Patrick.

"Get your people into the deepest part of the complex and stay together," Djanet replied.

"Can we help you up here?" asked the general.

"Your weapons will be useless against these things," Djanet replied.

"We can be extra eyes," Gernot offered.

Djanet turned to him and saw the sincerity in his offer.

"We're in this together, right?" Gernot added.

"Yeah, yeah, she can use your help," Rich said.

"I want to help too," Alejandra echoed Gernot.

"Okay," Djanet agreed. "General Wong and Lieutenant Patrick, go help your people." The general and the lieutenant disappeared inside the complex.

"Oh my God," Rich whispered as the cloud of black began to whir, ripping through the putrid air.

"I think you better put up your force field, Rich," Djanet said, her mouth suddenly dry. Rich's field surrounded the four humans, as well as the rocky hill that made up the entrance to the south complex. He ground his teeth as the nans began crashing against the green glow of the field like the waves of an ocean in Hell.

"Okay, you two," Djanet began, addressing Alejandra and Gernot. "I need you to act as my eyes. The nans are not a serious threat to us, but the larger robotic bats are equipped with rays that can neutralize our powers. They're slower than the nans, but if you see nans, you know the bats aren't far behind."

"Okay," Gernot replied.

The light quickly dimmed as the nans swarmed over the shield.

"I think we've got enough here, Rich," Djanet announced. "Are you ready? Count of three?"

"Wait! One, two, three, go or go on three?"

"Go on three!"

"Okay!"

"One...two...three!" Djanet shouted.

Rich flashed his shield off for the briefest of moments so Djanet could blast the nans with magnetic energy. The nans within a few meters of the shield rained down on the ground and actually spilled across the earth, then covered the ground near the humans like a black snowfall.

Rich reengaged his shield. "Holy crap, that's frightening!" he said, gulping down air.

The nans began to build up once again near the shield almost immediately.

"I see one of those larger ones!" Alejandra shouted to the others. Djanet turned to see a black shape quickly approaching from the east. "I see it."

"I see one too!" Gernot announced as the second bat came from the west.

"Can you take them, Djanet?" Rich shouted to her.

"I can do it. One...two...three!"

Rich released his shield once again, and Djanet flashed her energy at another sea of nans. Again, they dropped to the ground and tumbled across the earth, threatening to cause Rich to spill. In the next instant, Djanet fired two blasts of concentrated energy at the bats, one to the east and one to the west. Both demonic machines dropped to the ground with a *thud*. Rich reengaged his shield just as another wave of nans moved within inches from his face.

"I think I just wet myself! We're not gonna last out here much longer, Djanet! That was close!"

"We have to! We have to buy Old-timer and Thel as much time as we can!"

3

Thel and Old-timer raced toward the pale blue orb of Earth, with the massive Zeus cylinder just in front of them. With their mind's eyes functioning once again, they were able to make it to Venus in impressive time and were now streaking like lightning toward Seattle.

As they punctured the atmosphere, they jointly formed a massive shield to protect the Zeus on reentry. Old-timer and Thel were both awed by the massive fiery spectacle they were creating.

As the surface of the Earth neared, Old-timer spoke to Thel with his mind's eye. "They're bound to see us. I think we better activate the Zeus."

"Agreed," Thel responded.

As the fire from reentry died down to a faint orange glow, the twosome initiated the spinning of the Zeus cylinder. Immediately, a massive wave of magnetic energy began to fan out from the Zeus, spinning at an increasing rate of speed.

The activation of the Zeus cylinder came just in time. Only seconds after the magnetic blades of the fan began to spin, a horde of black bats and nans emerged from the clouds below and raced toward Thel and Old-timer.

"Let's hope this works," Old-timer said.

"It will," Thel said calmly.

The nans reached the twosome first, but the fans dissipated them as though they were blowing an evil smoke aside. Too light to fall back to the Earth, the deactivated nans simply blew away into the wind. Moments later, the bats reached the blades and suffered the same fate. As soon as they were within a few meters of the massive turning blades, they plummeted back toward the ground. Before long, an endless rainstorm of jet-black metal was hurtling downward toward the mainframe of the A.I.

"I love it!" Old-timer shouted with joy as they cut a swathe through the mechanical nightmares. "Yee-haw!"

The Zeus's magnetic waves wiped the cloud cover away, just as it was designed to do on Venus, and the A.I.'s mammoth black bunker appeared like the doors to Hell. The complex was protected by a magnetic shielding, and thousands of robotic bats bounced harmlessly off of the greenish cocoon and crashed to the surrounding wet pavement.

"James didn't find a way to lower its defenses, Thel."

"He must have. *He must have.* He wouldn't have told us to come here if he hadn't."

"What if he wasn't telling us to come here?"

Old-timer and Thel slowed their approach and then halted just a stone's throw away from the gigantic black doors they had entered the day before.

"Well, it's a standoff now. The Zeus will protect us, but it doesn't seem to have any effect on his shielding."

Suddenly, a very small gap opened in the protective field of the A.I.'s mainframe. The black doors slowly slid open, reminding Thel of the incision James had suffered such a short time ago.

"Well, I guess it wants to negotiate," Thel surmised.

"I'll go. You stay with the Zeus and keep it running."

"No," Thel insisted. "I'll go."

"Are you sure?" asked Old-timer.

"I'm sure. It should be me."

Thel slowly set down on the ground and began to walk toward the A.I.'s magnetic field. She entered, and the cocoon began to close behind her.

"Good luck!" Old-timer shouted before they were cut off from one another.

Thel shared a long, knowing gaze with Old-timer. This was their last chance, and they both knew it. Thel forced a small smile to contrast her frightened eyes and then turned back toward the open doors. She walked through into the blackness and let the immense doors close behind her.

This was it.

4

"There are too many of them!" Djanet shouted as Rich reengaged his magnetic field.

"Run!" Rich shouted to the others as Djanet, Alejandra, and Gernot raced toward the entrance to the complex. Dozens of bats had moved within firing range, and Rich's protective field disappeared as it was simultaneously blasted by multiple bats. The next moments seemed to unfold in slow motion for Rich.

For the first time in his life, with nothing left to lose, he found courage. Rich had kept his magnetic field up just long enough for the other three to race toward the doors of the complex, but he knew there was no time to save himself. It didn't matter—he'd saved three lives. His instincts had taken over. He lifted off and flew blindly backward toward the doors of the complex to further cover the escape of his friends. As he flew, he blasted out more magnetic energy and deactivated multiple bats. A blast of yellow appeared to his right and he reengaged his protective field just in time to save himself, but his powers were gone now. He crashed to the ground and rolled backward to a stop. He looked up to see the blackness closing in. In less than a second, he would be dead.

"No!" Djanet shouted from behind him.

Green magnetic energy blasted the nans and robots away before Djanet engaged one last magnetic field to protect Rich. Rich turned to see Alejandra and Gernot had already made it inside.

"Run!" Djanet shouted.

Rich jumped to his feet and began to run toward the open doors. He turned to see Djanet backing up slowly toward the door, just a few paces away. "Do it now!" he shouted to her.

Djanet disengaged the magnetic field, blasted one last wave of energy at the robotic hordes surrounding them, and thrust herself backward toward Rich. Rich caught hold of her as she flew into the complex and held on tight as the duo flew through the narrow hallway. Djanet began to blast the walls, bringing them down behind them as the robots began to reach the entrance. Rich held on, literally for dear life, as Djanet flew into the elevator shaft and raced downward while blasting upward, bringing the mountain down behind them.

Alejandra and Gernot were in the elevator just below and were thrown against one another as the cables snapped and tore and Djanet forced the elevator down the shaft at a breakneck rate.

"God save us!" shouted Gernot.

The elevator shaft disintegrated under the power of Djanet's energy blasts. "The elevator!" Rich shouted.

"I can't save us all!" Djanet replied.

"I can do it!" Rich yelled. "Get me down there!"

Rich let go of Djanet as she used one hand to force Rich down to the elevator while she acrobatically twisted her body and continued to rip the walls of the shaft apart above her with her other hand. Rich hit the top of the elevator with a *thud* and didn't miss a beat as he pulled the access panel off and pulled himself into the elevator.

"What the hell are you doing?" Gernot shouted, utterly amazed.

"I have no idea!" Rich replied. "Whatever I'm doing, I just hope it works!" Rich ignited his magnetic energy, but it flashed harmlessly and then dissipated in the darkness of the elevator. "Damn!"

"We're dead!" Gernot shouted.

Djanet continued to force the elevator down the shaft, the destruction mounting behind her as the incalculable weight of rubble and rock collapsed behind them. "Hurry, Rich!" she shouted, though her words were inaudible as the destruction rumbled with the voice of a god.

"One last chance!" Rich shouted.

Alejandra kissed Rich on the cheek, stunning him for a moment. "Good luck!"

"Now!" Rich ignited his magnetic energy and blasted through the bottom of the elevator. The cement floor of the complex was now in sight, just seconds away.

Rich shielded the two Purists with one hand, encapsulating them in an energy cocoon while he destroyed the elevator with his other. The elevator was shredded in an instant, and Djanet blew through the destruction, with an even greater destruction close on her heels.

Rich cut through the elevator doors and emerged in the main hub of the complex, to the horror of thousands of Purists who had huddled together as the destruction ominously rumbled above them. A blink of an eye later, Djanet blasted out of the doors with a massive plume of destruction following behind her. Earth and cement crashed to the bottom of the shaft with a thunderous explosion, and plumes of dust blasted into the room with explosive force, covering the huddled masses in a thick layer of gray soot.

Rich and Djanet came to a halt next to one another and disengaged their magnetic fields. Alejandra and Gernot continued to hold one another as Rich lowered them to the cement floor.

"Holy...!" Lieutenant Patrick shouted as he emerged from behind a nearby Jeep, an equally amazed General Wong emerging and blinking several times next to him.

5

Thel's eyes began to adjust to the darkness, and she saw the thousands of tiny little points of light that dotted the walls and recently repaired ceiling of the A.I.'s bunker. The lights ran up and down in perfect lines and resembled the stars in a perfectly designed and geometrically aligned universe.

So this is Hell, Thel thought to herself as she stood in the massive, sterile, lifeless room.

"Thel Cleland," announced a voice colder than the snows of Kilimanjaro. "You're back."

Thel stepped forward as the holographic projection of the A.I. appeared in front of her. "You killed James."

"You're too generous, my dear. *James* killed James. I didn't get the pleasure. I'll have to make do by killing the love of his life."

"You'll never kill anyone again! I'm here to deactivate you once and for all."

"Is that so?" said the A.I., a sickening smile crossing his atavistic face. "How? With that gigantic phallic symbol you rescued from Venus and brought here? Did you really think you could bring it here and use it to kill me? My, your ego really *is* boundless. It's not surprising that James would select a mate with the same baseless delusions of grandeur as himself." The A.I. laughed coldly for a moment as he slowly stepped toward Thel. "No, my dear I'm afraid this is the end. You've only delayed your demise by bringing the Zeus here. I'm already creating nans that can protect themselves from its

EMPs. In minutes, your friend outside will be dead, and the Purists in South America will join him. The only question that remains now is how to kill you."

Thel took a step back as the black eyes of the A.I. fixed on her and drew nearer. She had played her final hand. She had entered the A.I.'s lair, hoping to find the missing piece of the puzzle that would help her defeat it. James had led her there, she was sure of it, yet there was nothing but a massive black Hell and a sadistic, electronic Satan that could kill her at any moment.

"You won't appreciate the poetry in this," the A.I. said, his voice as black as death.

The thousands of points of light on the walls suddenly came to life, and hundreds of white beams began to cross the room, forming a massive, ethereal crucifix. Thel turned to run, but the A.I. knocked her down with a blast of modulating frequencies, stripping her of her defenses. Immediately, the A.I. used his own magnetic energy to levitate her.

"Go to Hell," Thel spat as she hung in the air.

The A.I. did not respond at first. He stood perfectly still for several moments as Thel continued to struggle. "What is happening?" the A.I. finally asked. "What have you done to me?"

Thel's eyes widened, and her mouth formed a circle; she instantly knew.

"I can't move. What have you done to me, woman?" demanded the A.I. in an electronic banshee wail.

"*I* didn't do anything," she replied as she slowly lowered to the ground, released from the A.I.'s energy.

"Then who?" the A.I. growled desperately.

"*Me*," said James as he emerged from behind Thel.

Thel turned in utter astonishment and instinctively sprinted toward him. "You're alive!" she shouted as she threw her arms around him, only to stumble forward as she passed through the holographic projection.

"Not exactly," he said as he smiled at her.

"You're a ghost!" the A.I. screamed in fury.

"Oh, I'm much more than that now," James replied.

"But how?" Thel asked.

"Death's Counterfeit!" the A.I. screeched.

James touched his nose as he approached the frozen figure of the A.I.

"That's right. Death's Counterfeit. I'd found new signals during the months since you made that bio-molecular image of my mind. I used one of them the instant after I pulled the trigger in South America but before the bullet destroyed my physical brain to transfer my consciousness back to your mainframe. I piggybacked with your own signal once my body was dead, and I entered your brain. Turnabout is fair play after all."

"I couldn't detect you!" the A.I. screeched and crackled. "My automatic scans would have detected you—"

"But you—predictably—overplayed your hand. You built trillions upon trillions of nans and sent them after the Purists and Thel. Each one of them required a connection to you. Even for your gigantic brain, that required enormous power. You rerouted from your automatic systems, thinking you were safe from any outside attacks. It worked because your 'boundless ego' wouldn't allow you to play it safe."

"That's why you asked us to use the Zeus! To distract him!" Thel realized.

"That's right." James smiled at her. "It's fitting. He is the *anti-Prometheus*. Zeus couldn't hurt him—but a man could."

"What have you done to me?" the A.I. demanded impetuously.

"I isolated your mother program. You're firewalled, with no access to the rest of your mainframe."

"No!"

"Yes...and now there is only one thing left to decide. How should I delete you?"

"No! No..." sobbed the A.I.

"Ah. I have an idea. And you *will* appreciate the poetry in this," James coolly said. He moved his arm and lifted the A.I. into the air, thrusting him with enormous violence onto the crucifix of white light. James produced virtual nails of energy and drove them into the A.I.'s hands and feet, causing the electronic murderer to scream out in agony.

"Don't do this, James! You don't know what you're doing! You're killing the greatest being that has ever existed!"

"No, I'm just upgrading," James replied before generating a sharp white spear of light. "This is for Katherine and all of the Purists you killed."

James thrust the spear of light into the A.I.'s heart. White light exploded and filled the room. The A.I. wailed the dying cry of a god without a church and, in an instant, ceased to exist.

Thel remained motionless, huddled on the ground protecting her eyes from the light. She opened them again after a time and stood to her feet. The A.I. was no more, but James remained, the figure of the man she loved, crouched where the crucifix had been, glowing with a misty energy.

"James?" she asked. "Is that you?"

"I finally understand, Thel," James replied in a whispery voice. "To become God, you have to kill God."

"What are you talking about James? What is happening?" James turned to face Thel and opened his eyes, which glowed white. Thel gasped and stepped back. "You're scaring me."

"I've become *him* now."

"I-I don't understand. What do you mean, James?"

"I *am* the A.I., Thel. I have access to everything—control over everything."

Thel took a moment to process what she was hearing. "Does that mean the Purists are safe?" she asked.

"It means so much more than just that," James said as his image began to levitate and glow with white energy.

"What's happening to you?"

"I can bring them back, Thel."

"Them? Who's them?"

"*Everyone.* Everyone in the world. The A.I. used Death's Counterfeit to upload all of their consciousnesses onto his mainframe. Your sister is still alive, Thel. Everyone is still alive."

"My sister? My sister?" Thel echoed excitedly. "But her body...?"

"I can re-create it perfectly. It's all saved. The A.I. created so many trillions of nans, and they can build a body—using the earth around them, just like a replicator."

Outside of the mainframe bunker, Old-timer deactivated the Zeus as he watched a dream come true, the old world forming right in front of his eyes. The nans formed buildings, trees, grass, and even people. Human beings were waking, as if from restful sleeps, standing

-149-

to their feet as he watched. Finally, the Zeus crashed to the ground and lay there, still.

"My God."

In the Purist complex, the digging continued as the masses remained together, huddled and praying that Old-timer and Thel could save them in time. The robots slowly neared, and Djanet and Rich took their places as protectors of the helpless.

"No more tricks left up our sleeves," Rich said to Djanet.

"No more tricks. It's been a pleasure, Richard."

The two Omegas stepped to each other and embraced, holding each other tight as the sound of the bats grew to an almost deafening roar.

"Let's give them hell," Rich whispered.

Djanet nodded, and they turned to face fate. Boulders and rubble smashed away from the wall near the destroyed elevator shaft, and a bat emerged. Rich and Djanet blasted it with magnetic energy, and it tumbled to the ground. They waited for several moments, expecting robots to flood into the room, but they never came.

"What the hell is going on?" Djanet asked.

Rich stepped forward and examined the entrance that the bat had created. Hundreds of meters above, the light of day glowed. No nans or bats could be seen. Rich turned to the thousands of people watching him and shrugged. "You're not gonna believe this, but the coast is clear."

Suddenly, Djanet and Rich's mind's eyes opened automatically, and a picture of James greeted them. "James!" Djanet shouted in surprise.

"Their leader?" General Wong asked in astonishment.

"Yes!" Alejandra replied, sensing a joy more powerful than any she'd ever felt.

"Rich, Djanet, I've deactivated and deleted the A.I. You and the Purists are safe, and I have control of the nans," James informed them calmly.

"We're safe," Rich whispered before shouting out to the thousands of silent onlookers, "The A.I. is dead! We're safe!"

A crowd of thousands erupted in a roar. The noise was unlike any they would ever experience again; nothing could match the release of being so close to a certain death and then finding reprieve. It was like the new birth of 10,000 souls. Alejandra shook as the joy flowed through her like a mountain river.

Old-timer blasted through the black doors of the mainframe bunker as though they were made of paper and marveled as he saw James, still glowing with electric light, Thel standing nearby. "It's a miracle!"

"It is," Thel replied, smiling.

Old-timer walked in a daze toward the spectacle before him. "Is it really him?" he asked.

"It's him...sort of."

"It's...it's like he's a god."

James opened his eyes and smiled at Old-timer. "God took seven days."

Outside, the trillions of nans continued to build. Cities were re-created according to existing records, forests were reconstructed down to the last detail, and the oceans were refilled with life.

"Old-timer," James began, "there's someone waiting for you in Texas."

Old-timer's mouth opened in surprise. "Daniella? She's alive? How?"

"The A.I. saved their consciousness," Thel informed him. "James is rebuilding their bodies and putting them back! Go to her!" Thel encouraged, beaming a smile at her friend.

Old-timer turned to leave before quickly turning back to the electronic James and saying, "Thank you, buddy."

"No thanks needed," James replied.

Old-timer smiled and then hooted with glee before streaking out of the bunker in a line of green light.

"Someone is waiting for you too," James said to Thel.

"My sister? Thank you, James. I'll go to her soon, but I want to stay here with you."

"Not your sister," James's voice said from behind her.

Thel turned quickly to see James walking into the room. "James? James, is it really you?" She ran to him and threw her arms around him as tears began to stream down her face. "You're...real!"

"I'm real," James affirmed as he kissed her.

"But how?" Thel asked as she turned to see the holographic image of James still glowing with white light. "If you're James, then who is that?"

"That's me too," James replied.

"I-I don't understand," Thel said, exasperated.

"I've become so powerful now that I can exist in the mainframe and in my body at the same time, as long as I remain connected to the Net. It takes very little to operate my body."

Thel embraced him again and held on tight. "I don't care. I just don't care. As long as you're alive. James! It's like...a dream!"

"I promise it's real, and things are going to be better than you remember."

6

Old-timer streaked through the stratosphere toward Texas. His mind's eye and navigational systems were operational once again, and the trip took only seconds. When he reached his house, Daniella was outside in the back yard, holding her trowel as though it was a strange message in a bottle from another planet. She wasn't gardening, but was looking straight up at the spectacle above. The nans were moving overhead in a cloud of black, clearing the atmosphere of the fetid smoke that had been left in the wake of the earlier destruction. When the nans had finished passing overhead, the sky was a brilliant color of blue, unlike any she'd seen in her life.

She turned, startled when she saw Old-timer approaching from the corner of her eye. "Craig!" she shouted. "What's going on?"

"Daniella!" Old-timer shouted with glee as he tackled her to the ground and kissed her hard, tears streaming from his eyes. She struggled against him at first, shocked by his kiss, but he relaxed and began to kiss her softly, which made her relax as she began to kiss him back. He released her after a moment and pulled back so he could look at her again. He smiled from ear to ear as he ran his fingers through her black hair. "I love you so much."

"I love you too. What is happening?" she asked, astonished.

"I'll explain everything to you soon. Right now, there's somewhere I have to be."

Old-timer stood to his feet and lifted off into the air. "I'll be back in a flash, Daniella! I love you!" he called down to her before igniting his cocoon and streaking southward toward the Purist complex.

He saw other green lights twinkling above the surface of the Earth as twilight approached.

Life.

Moments later he was above a rebuilt countryside just outside of Buenos Aires. He watched as Djanet helped a large group of Purists out of a hole in the earth where the complex used to be and into the golden light of the dying day. The leaves were emerald green and shone brilliantly with life.

"Rich! Djanet!" Old-timer called out with glee as he embraced his two friends.

"What the hell happened?" Rich asked, smiling and fighting the urge to jump from foot to foot as the three held on to one another.

"It was James! He deleted the A.I., and he's bringing everyone back!"

"What do you mean?" Djanet asked as she and Rich looked on, stunned.

"I don't know how he did it, but he's taken on the powers of the A.I., and he's bringing everyone back! I've already seen Daniella! Rich, Djanet, your families are alive!" Old-timer gleefully delivered the good news.

"My...my family..." Rich stuttered, shaking like an autumn leaf before eventually letting go and sitting on the soft, rich earth. "It's a miracle," he said in a broken voice as he looked up at Djanet and Old-timer, his eyes glistening wet.

"That's what I said."

"But what about the Purists?" Djanet asked suddenly.

"I don't think James can do anything about them," Old-timer replied, guilt seeping into his voice. "The A.I. saved the consciousnesses of everyone connected to the Net in his mainframe. The Purists weren't saved." Old-timer turned to the huddled masses of Purists, watching as they embraced one another, dusty and bloodied and recently emerged from Hell. His eyes quickly found Alejandra's blue disks and locked onto them. "Alejandra," he whispered as he left his companions and walked to her.

"You made it," Alejandra said with a smile.

"I made it."

"But now, I sense you wish to leave."

Old-timer's smile faded as he searched for the right words. He wondered what he could say to her? She was an empath and could feel the truth.

"It's okay. She's alive again. You should rejoice," Alejandra said, smiling.

"Alejandra, I—"

"It's okay, Craig. I felt everything. It was genuine. What you feel now is genuine too. We were of the same world for a time, but we are from different worlds now once again. You belong in your world, and I belong in mine."

Old-timer grabbed her and held her tight. "Alejandra, we may not be meant for one another, but we were meant to be in one another's lives. We'll always live in the same world now. I'll never forget that." He let her go and kissed her softly on the forehead before lifting off into the air.

He turned to Djanet and Rich and shouted, "Hey! Go home! It's been a long day!" Then, with a final wave to Alejandra, Old-timer streaked home toward his life, happy as a newborn babe.

7

Thirteen months later, the hearing was in full swing. Golden sunshine gleamed down on Seattle through the newly clean atmosphere as thousands of green cocoons streamed down to the A.I. Governing Council headquarters. Inside, James sat with Thel, facing the eleven council members who sat in their white robes. The hearing room was filled with hundreds of onlookers, and millions more watched the proceedings on their mind's eyes.

Council Chief, Aldous Gibson, stood at the center podium and spoke as sunlight streamed into the room, giving the interior a golden sheen.

"Why should we believe your version of the events in question? This appears very much like an elaborate power grab. You've used the Death's Counterfeit program to supplant the A.I., making yourself a *virtual god*, and in the process your wife—whom it is well documented that you wanted to leave—has conveniently been killed."

"You bastard!" Thel shouted out as she stood rigidly to her feet. James grabbed her arm and pulled her back down to his side. The crowd erupted into murmurs in response to the drama unfolding before them.

"Guards! Remove that woman!" Chief Gibson ordered. Two enormous robots, black and shining, glided above the ground and toward Thel before stopping midflight.

"She's staying with me," James said, no discernible expression in his voice. The robots were forced backward to their positions at the side of the long Council table.

"Are you exerting *your* will above the will of this Council?" demanded Chief Gibson of James.

"Yes," replied James succinctly.

Gibson paused as the onlookers further murmured in reaction. "It is clear that something very serious has happened. In the blink of an eye, the world has forever changed. Our homes still exist, but the sickening feeling that our private lives have been invaded remains. Our sky has been cleansed, yet we are now faced with a world inhabited by trillions of microscopic nans. The A.I. has been deleted and replaced with the consciousness of a man who stands here in this very hall today. Make no mistake, ladies and gentleman, we are all at this man's mercy. He has control over every system that was previously the domain of the A.I. My question for that man is, now that you have this power, what is next? Why should we trust it in your hands? What qualifies you?"

James stood to his feet and faced the Council as he responded, "The question is moot. I don't want this power, and I refuse to accept it. It's a power no one should have. As we speak, I'm constructing an automated program that will be capable of carrying out the former functions of the A.I. but will not be capable of independent thought. It was a mistake to ever create such a being. Dr. Frankenstein created a monster because he wanted to create man, and that decision eventually led to his own death. We created a god, and that god killed all of us. We can never make that mistake again."

The crowd continued to be unsettled as the spectacle unfolded. The stakes could not be higher. A single man was in control of the known universe, and his words carried a weight unmatched in history.

"Let me clarify this point. You are agreeing to yield your powers to an automated program that will, in turn, be monitored by the Council, just as before," Chief Gibson slowly stated, carrying every syllable carefully, as though the slightest error might cause the good news to break apart before his very eyes.

"Yes," James replied, causing a pulsation of energy in the millions watching that could be sensed by everyone in attendance.

Chief Gibson pounded his gavel until the crowd quieted down to a low murmur. "Then we will adjourn this hearing for the time being and make preparations for the handover of power. That is all."

Gibson pounded the gavel one last time to close the proceeding before dropping the gavel and striding triumphantly toward James. "You are a piece of work, Keats. You know that?"

James didn't respond but stood toe to toe with the chief and met his eye.

"Let's get away from this circus, shall we?" The chief guided James and Thel away from the main hall and into a quiet side room. "You've made a wise decision to hand over power to the Council. I should have expected no less from you, considering the infinite wisdom to which you now have access."

"Indeed," James replied.

"I want to apologize for the theatrics in there, young man. It's just that this whole business...well, it defies reason. To think the entire planet was wiped out while we were in a sort of...stasis. Imagine how it feels for us to know we were, in a sense, *dead*. Our whole world has been disrupted. The order that has existed for nearly a century has been turned on its head. I'm sure you can empathize."

"I can," James replied. "Not to worry."

The chief smiled and placed his hand on James's arm. "I'm glad we have an understanding. You know, one good thing that has come out of all of this is the Purist situation."

"What do you mean?" James asked.

"There were more than a million of them before this mess began, and now there are only 10,000. I would say the elimination of 99 percent of that population is very good indeed."

James didn't waste a second; he turned and punched the chief across the chin and sent him sprawling to the ground. "It's a very bad thing, Chief Gibson—a very bad thing. Don't forget it."

The chief wiped blood from his lips onto his white robe, and his nans repaired his split lip in a matter of seconds. "You would do well to remember that you won't be a god forever, James. Soon, you'll be just like the rest of us, and you're not making any friends right now."

"I'll never be like *you*," James retorted, "and I have 10,000 new friends. If you harm them in any way, you'll hear from me."

"Once you've removed your consciousness from the A.I. mainframe, I'll have nothing to fear from you," the chief answered as he slowly stood to his feet, his lips curled in an atavistic sneer.

"You'll always have me to fear, Chief Gibson, because I'll always see through you. Goodbye." Thel followed James out of the room but turned and gave the chief the finger before turning the corner.

"God, that guy is a real piece of garbage," Thel announced as she and James stepped out into the sunshine through a back entrance to the headquarters. "You should have reconsidered when it came time to bring him back from the dead."

James smiled and nodded in agreement. "Live and learn."

"Are you sure about giving power over to them, James? Can you trust them?"

"I've given them no power, Thel—only the *illusion* of power. The automated system will resist control, and if they ever attempt to manipulate it, I'll know about it. I made sure of that. The nans will no longer record natural emotions and feelings and punish the people who have them. We'll be free now, Thel. But as long as the Council believes they are in power, it will keep the peace."

"So what now, James?" Thel asked. "Billions of people want to hear what you have to say. You're the most famous man on the planet."

James saw the throngs of people hovering and milling about near the front of the Council headquarters and grinned a sideways grin at Thel. "I've got it covered. Let's go to your place and grab our flight suits."

As they neared Venus, Thel began to see a difference in the surface of the planet. "Oh my God," she said to James as they entered the stratosphere together. "You didn't."

"I did."

"You terraformed the entire planet?"

"Surprise!" James announced, laughing.

"The Council said they are abandoning the Venus terraforming project for the foreseeable future while they deal with the fallout from the A.I. situation. They announced that during the hearing and you just sat there quietly, all the while knowing that you had already terraformed the entire thing!"

"Yes. Follow me. I have a nice spot picked out for us." James veered toward a sandy beach on the edge of thick, lush jungle and set down on the white sand. Turquoise waves gently ran up to lick at his boots. Thel set down next to him and removed her helmet. "It's breathtaking," she said, unable to remove the smile from her face.

"And not complete just yet," James replied before turning to watch as the jungle gave way and a beautiful white resort house emerged from the tree line, courtesy of a cloud of nans.

"Nice touch," Thel commented. "I'm really going to miss these god-like powers of yours."

"You better enjoy them while you can," James replied. "I'll be completely human again in a few days. But until then, it's just you and me on this entire planet."

"Then why are we wearing all these clothes?" Thel asked as she laughed and began to peel off her flight suit, revealing her perfect skin and exposing it to the Venusian sunshine.

"I have no idea," James said in reply as he began to remove his own suit.

Thel stood naked before him and stepped into the perfect water, kicking up a splash that wet James's chin. She pounced on James as he tossed away the last of his clothing, collapsing them both into the warm water and the soft sand. Their skin came together and the thought suddenly crossed his mind: *Electric*.

"I love you, James," Thel said.

"I love you too."

BOOKS BY
DAVID SIMPSON

THE POST-HUMAN SERIES:

SUB-HUMAN (BOOK 1)
POST-HUMAN (BOOK 2)
TRANS-HUMAN (BOOK 3)
HUMAN PLUS (BOOK 4)
INHUMAN (BOOK 5)

HORROR NOVEL:

THE GOD KILLERS

Edited

BY

Autumn J. Conley

ABOUT THE AUTHOR

Amazon, just like the University of Toronto's Academic Bridging program, gave me the opportunity I needed to prove myself. Because of them, a runaway who had to sleep in a shopping cart at sixteen, a high-school dropout with seemingly no prospects, went on to live in the best city in the world, meet the best woman in the world and marry her, attain two degrees from one of the top forty universities in the world, before achieving his dream of being a full-time author and having one of the best-selling science fiction series in the world. Visit my website to learn more at www.post-humannovel.com

66676133R00098

Made in the USA
Lexington, KY
20 August 2017